Humility's Burden

Daniel Stewart

WESTBOW PRESS®
A DIVISION OF THOMAS NELSON & ZONDERVAN

WestBow Press books may be ordered through booksellers or by contacting:

WestBow Press
A Division of Thomas Nelson & Zondervan
1663 Liberty Drive
Bloomington, IN 47403
www.westbowpress.com
1 (866) 928-1240

ISBN: 978-1-9736-3672-4 (sc)
ISBN: 978-1-9736-3673-1 (e)

Print information available on the last page.

WestBow Press rev. date: 8/9/2018

Contents

Chapter One

The City of Spirituality

She was a young woman dressed in dirty men's clothing from a dumpster and burdened by a large heavy suitcase she was dragging down a dark alley in the City of Spirituality. I should tell you how she got there, or you might mistake her for a homeless person, which wouldn't be accurate. A few moments earlier she was wearing a black skirt and a white silk blouse. However, those feminine clothes were stripped from her by the Shame Enforcement Officers. They threw her into a dumpster to teach her a lesson about her true spiritual role in society.

When crawling out of that nasty garbage (which is where she acquired and clothed herself with dirty men's clothing), she had to pull, twist, and jerk the large and heavy suitcase out of the dumpster, and then she hit the ground hard. Her clothes itched and smelled of shame, and her suitcase was full of heavy burdensome shame. But why did she have it? That is a good question. Why did she drag that suitcase full of burdensome shame out of the dumpster?

When she got out of the dumpster, the Shame Enforcement Officers were no longer present, for they never lingered longer than what was needed to shame someone. It's a busy job enforcing the laws of social status in the City of Spirituality, and especially when the city legislation keeps writing more laws each week. You can always count on the Shame Enforcement Officers to do their job as quick, efficient, and frequent as you might see a postman delivering the mail.

They treated this woman with no less haste and efficiency. Her name is Humility; a light skinned girl with dark hair. Her walk down that dark alley in the City of Spirituality (with her burdensome suitcase of shame), was the most miserable experience of her life. In the past, she had often worried about the day she might meet the dreaded Shame Enforcement Officers, but she never imagined it would be for this reason. Have you guessed why she was shamed? Let me give you a hint. In the City of Spirituality, it is against the laws of social status for a woman to speak or instruct on her own authority about matters of spiritual reality.

Humility never saw herself as spiritually authoritative. She had grown up in the City of Spirituality, where great and renowned spiritual men were the leaders, and women extended their authority no further than the reach of those men. Don't get me wrong, there were plenty of women who would lead, speak, and teach with spiritual authority, but if one of them ever did it in a way that made them appear greater, wiser, or more authoritative than a male spiritual leader, it would be a serious violation of the laws of social status.

Humility wasn't even a spiritual leader when she broke the law. Her parents had taught her the basics, but she learned most of what she knew by living in a city full to the brim with spirituality. Every coffee shop, book store, grocery mart, café, bar, business, and street corner expressed and influenced the diverse mystical reality of the City of Spirituality. But Humility was not that serious about it, and she wasn't even sure what she believed. She didn't belong to a particular group or church or religion or organization. Her belief was open, and she described herself as spiritual, but not religious.

So what happened? You must be wondering. How did this spiritually diverse average girl in her early twenties become a law breaker of social status? How did she extend her spiritual authority beyond the reach of the leading spiritual men in the city? When did she become so interested and concerned with spirituality that she would say something authoritative about it? She was, up to that point, an absorber of spiritual information only. She never answered questions from her own opinion. If someone asked her about something spiritual, she always referred to what someone else had told her, never as if it was her own idea.

But something changed, didn't it? It always does. People say they never see the change coming, but that's what makes life so exciting. The greatest legends are the ones where the hero seems to come out of nowhere. It catches everyone by surprise; the unlikely hero who seemed to have no real value or purpose in the big picture of things. Humility was just that type of person in the City of Spirituality. She was a little fish in a vast ocean, but even the smallest events can change the course of history.

I told you that she was dragging that burdensome suitcase of shame in a dark alley, and the reason it was dark was because it was just after 10 p.m. However, Humility's spiritual change began about 12 hours earlier. It was a Friday, the first of a three-day weekend, and she had suddenly woken up with an intense thirst for orange juice, but there was none in the fridge. On her way to the grocery mart on the corner, she was approached by an old woman asking for change.

"Sorry, I don't have any," said Humility.

"Then maybe I should give some to you," said the Beggar Lady, as she held out some quarters.

"Oh, no thank you," said Humility, turning to see the quarters, and then turning back around to go into the mini-mart.

"Too greedy to give me some change, and too full of yourself to take my change; I see, then it must be another kind of change that you don't have, and another kind of change that you need," shouted the Beggar Lady.

"What do you mean?" asked Humility, as she turned back around inside the entrance of the store and came back outside. "I'm sorry; I didn't mean to offend you. I just don't carry cash with me. What do you need the money for? Maybe I can buy you something in the store?"

"I don't need anything from you. It is you who needs something from me," said the Beggar Lady, as she again held out three quarters in her hand.

Humility gave her a long-confused look and said, "Alright, if you really want me to take them, I will."

"That's good," said the Beggar Lady. "I don't have much, but what I give is all I have."

"All you have," returned Humility. "I can't take it if it's all you have."

"Yes, take it," she replied. "It is for that reason that you should take it. You see, for me, the change represents all I have, and by giving it to you I demonstrate generosity, even though the amount of money is of little value to you. There are two kinds of change, isn't there? One has little value for you, but the other has great value for you, doesn't it?"

"It's a play off of words," said Humility. "The change is three quarters, which is money, but it's also a symbol of transformation. I suppose you think I'm the one who needs to change."

"Yes," said the Beggar Lady. "Look at one of the quarters, on the side that has the head. Do you see the four-word phrase to the right of it?"

"Yes," said Humility. "It says, 'IN GOD WE TRUST.'"

"That's right," said the Beggar Lady. "But who or what does it mean by God? Is it suggesting that it is in the quarter or money itself that we should trust as God? Or is it suggesting that we should trust in the government or the president as God? Or is it suggesting that we should put our trust in something or someone else to be our God?"

"I don't know," said Humility. "That's a spiritual idea I've never thought about before."

"Keep those three quarters in your right hand for the rest of the day," said the Beggar Lady. "If you do you will have both kinds of change."

"I'm not really sure I want it," said Humility.

"You do," replied the Beggar Lady.

"Alright, but..." said Humility, but she was interrupted.

"I have to go; I'm late," shouted the Beggar Lady. And then she took off suddenly around the corner and was gone.

About ten hours later, Humility was in the city square with her best friend, Modesty, and to their surprise, there was a spiritual festival going on. The first booth they went to was a psychic palm reader, and how surprised was the woman, when she opened Humility's palm to read it, and saw three quarters. She jumped back in her seat and refused to read Humility's fortune. Modesty and Humility were both shocked at the fortune reader's response, but Modesty was confused as to why her best friend suddenly became so irritated by the palm reader's rejection and refused to explain why she had three quarters in her hand.

Then, in the midst of the large crowd forming around a stage, a mystical man, calling himself the Greatest Magician in the City of Spirituality, began his routine by asking a volunteer to come up on stage and assist him. Humility was mortified when he pointed to her and called her out in front of hundreds of people. She tried to disappear in the crowd, but everyone around her began moving away from her, and a large opening suddenly exposed her to where there was no getting away. She reluctantly climbed onto the stage.

"Yes, very good, brave girl," said the Magician. "Let's begin. Would you hold out your hands for me, please, arms stretched, and palms up?"

Humility did as he instructed, and when he saw the three coins, he told her to put them in her pocket. "I can't," she said. And being a superb showman, the Magician realized the imminent probability of an awkward moment (which he always avoided like the plague), so he chose to play along as if it was a part of the show.

"Of course you can't," he pronounced, in the tone of a gameshow host. "But please, tell our curious audience why you cannot put those coins in your pocket."

"Because a beggar lady told me this morning that I had to keep them inside my hand for the rest of the day," explained Humility.

"And did she tell you the reason for this mysterious assignment? Or perhaps she mistook you for a stock market investor. Or perhaps you really are one. Ladies and gentlemen, we might have here the

CEO of the first beggar investment firm," said the Magician, as the audience roared in laughter.

"That's not..." said Humility, in a barely audible voice, but she was interrupted.

"I'm just kidding, please, tell us, what else did the beggar lady say?" pronounced the Magician.

"She asked me what the quarter said on the right side of the head, and I read the words, 'IN GOD WE TRUST.' But then she asked me what it meant by God? Are we supposed to trust in money as our God, the government as our God, or something else as our God?" said Humility.

"And what did you say?" questioned the Magician.

"I said I didn't know," returned Humility.

"Well, today is your lucky day," he proclaimed to the audience. "It just so happens that I am a member of the council of this great City of Spirituality, and as an authoritative expert on the subject, I can tell you that 'IN GOD WE TRUST,' means that we should trust in our government, this great City of Spirituality, as our God."

"But couldn't it also mean that we should trust money as our God?" asked Humility. When she said this, the entire crowd gasped and then went completely silent.

"That's alright," announced the Magician to the audience. "She's not questioning my authority, she is just curious about what my opinion is on the possibility that it may be interpreted another way. Isn't that right, young lady?"

"Well..." she returned, but he cut her off out of fear that she would say the wrong thing and cross the line.

"Money has its purpose, yes, but this great City of Spirituality is far more trustworthy, for it is our sustainer and provider," proclaimed the Magician.

"But couldn't God mean something else besides money or the government?" questioned Humility.

"Something else; girl, there is nothing else," he returned. "People have debated for thousands of years as to who or what is God, but this great City of Spirituality has solved that question without a doubt. We are God. And it is this government, in which it stands, that protects and upholds spiritual diversity and pluralism, and so it is it that is God. It is in the City of Spirituality that we trust. Girl; seriously, think about what you are saying. What else could it mean?"

"I don't know, let me see, maybe, a Creator, who is the origin of everything we call good in the universe," said Humility.

"It sounds like you're questioning my authority," said the Magician. "I think our time here is finished, girl. Please, exit my stage."

About two hours later, after Humility and Modesty explored more of the spiritual festival, the Shame Enforcement Officers found the two girls a few blocks away. They let Modesty go without being shamed, but Humility had to suffer the consequences of her crime. And that is how it all began. Humility dragged her heavy Suitcase of Shame to the end of the dark alley in the City of Spirituality. When she turned onto the sidewalk of 5th Avenue, it was packed with people coming from the Spiritual Festival. The first 20 walkers gave her sad and pitiful looks, but the next 20 or so laughed at her in the cruelest ways. Every group has a leader, and the next one to pass on the sidewalk was led by a proud ridiculer who recognized Humility as the girl on the Magician's stage.

"Look who it is," said the Ridiculer. "It's the girl who made a fool of herself."

"No way, you're right," said the Ridiculer's Girlfriend. "Look at her; she's wearing dirty men's clothing, and she stinks."

"She was shamed," said a man.

"She deserved it, too," said another man.

"You're pathetic," shouted a woman at Humility.

"Where are you going, Garbage girl?" questioned the Ridiculer's Girlfriend. "You were hideous on that stage, you know. You disgraced yourself as a woman. It's poetic justice that you're wearing stinky, nasty, filthy men's clothing. If you want to speak like a man and debate men about spiritual reality, as other men do, then you should dress like a man."

"But if she is dressed like a man, then how fitting it should be that it be as a shameful loser," said the Ridiculer. "And look how she drags that hideous heavy suitcase of shame around with her. What do you have in there?"

"Don't touch it," shouted Humility, as the Ridiculer tried to open her Suitcase of Shame.

"The mangy mutt has rabies," pronounced the Ridiculer's Girlfriend, as she slapped Humility so hard across the face that she was knocked down. The rest of the crowd of people began spitting on her, and the Ridiculer opened her Suitcase of Shame.

"Look at this," proclaimed the Ridiculer. "How pathetic; look everybody. Do you see what she has in her Suitcase of Shame; books."

"What are you talking about?" said Humility. "Those aren't mine."

"What a loser," laughed the Ridiculer's Girlfriend. "What kind of books are they?"

"Let me see," said the Ridiculer, as he listed off the titles. Humility tried to stop him, but a large crowd of people had now formed on the sidewalk, and some of them held her back from interfering. "The Holy Bible; Systematic Theology; New Testament Commentary; Dictionary of Theology; Old Testament Commentary; History of Christianity, and a bunch of other Christian theology books. She dreams of being a theologian."

"What a loser," laughed the Ridiculer's Girlfriend. "Now we know why you questioned the Magician, don't we? You're learning from these books, and you think that gives you the right to have spiritual authority over a man; your punishment is not severe enough, I think. You should be beaten with those books."

"They're not my books," shouted Humility.

"Lier," shouted several people in the crowd. Suddenly, the Shame Enforcement Officers were present.

"What's going on here?" questioned one of the officers. "Leave this girl alone; move on, all of you."

"They're not my books," pleaded Humility to the people as they walked away.

"Hey girl, don't instigate them. Pack up your stuff and go home," said the Shame Enforcement Officer.

"They're not mine," said Humility.

"I saw you pull that suitcase out of the dumpster, not twenty minutes ago," he returned. "It's yours, and I don't want to hear anything else about it. Pack it up and go."

She did as he said and dragged her suitcase of shame a mile through town until she arrived home. Are you wondering why a suitcase of theology books would be associated with shame? I will tell you. In the City of Spirituality, only some older women are permitted to exercise spiritual authority, and only when it's teamed up with the greater authority of a spiritual man. However, if a young woman shows the intent to learn spirituality on her own (without men), and then use her gained knowledge as spiritual authority over men, she is viewed by the people as bad hygiene for society. It's as if her spiritual authority is the stinky contamination of sewage.

Therefore, those theology books in the suitcase are shameful because the use of them by a young woman to gain spiritual knowledge and authority is shameful, not because the books themselves are shameful. Humility knew this, and for that reason she didn't want them, but she couldn't get rid of them. When the Shame Enforcement Officers threw her into that dumpster they cursed her with a spell that she would have to keep whatever shameful thing she found in the dumpster.

It was an hour before midnight when she got home and realized that the longer she held the handle of the suitcase, it became fused to her hand, as if she was superglued to it. This caused her to panic and lose control of her temper; cussing, kicking things, and screaming. She lived in an apartment building, and she finally stopped when the neighbors on both sides were shouting back and banging on the walls for her to stop.

After she calmed down, and silently contemplated the cursed suitcase for a moment, with its handle in her left hand, she opened her right hand and saw the three quarters. She didn't like seeing them again and was annoyed that she was still holding them. She swung her arm back to throw the coins across the room, but then stopped when an idea suddenly came to mind. She wondered if the old beggar lady knew something was going to happen. She told Humility that if she held onto the coins for the rest of the day, she would experience some kind of change, but she didn't say exactly what it would be.

And here she was, just before midnight, with the quarters still in her right hand, and look what has happened since. Do you see what those quarters have caused to take place? She thought about how she had been shamed because of the questions she had asked the Magician; questions about the coins. Did the beggar lady know she was going to be shamed? Was that the change she was referring to? Why would anyone wish something so evil to happen to someone?

"Read the coins again," whispered a voice.

"Someone here?" returned Humility, as she turned around in all directions to see if someone was in her apartment.

"Read it again," whispered the voice.

"Who are you?" repeated Humility.

"What does it say?" whispered the voice again.

"IN GOD WE TRUST," said Humility. "Is this the answer to my question? Are you God? Am I supposed to trust in you? Are you God? Why aren't you answering me?"

She didn't get the response she wanted, but then suddenly the suitcase handle released from her grasp and sprung open as it fell to the floor. Humility picked up the Bible and read, "The LORD, the LORD, a God merciful and gracious, slow to anger, and abounding in steadfast love and faithfulness, keeping steadfast love for thousands, forgiving iniquity and transgression and sin, but who will by no means clear the guilty."

The next day she was no longer wearing those dreadful men's clothing, but simple jeans and a t-shirt, for it was a warm summer afternoon. However, she was still dragging her burdensome suitcase of shame, because the curse of the Shame Enforcement Officers had not been broken, and she couldn't get rid of the suitcase. She tried to throw it away or leave it behind, but something like an invisible force compelled her against her will to take the suitcase wherever she went.

"Where have you been?" questioned Modesty, who appeared suddenly outside the apartment. "I was so worried about you. I called you, I knocked on your door, and you were nowhere. What happened last night? Did they shame you? Why are you dragging that suitcase? What's in it; stones?"

"Alright, Modesty, I get it. You have questions, and you want me to give you answers," said Humility. "I don't see why I should have to answer you."

"You're upset, because I didn't stay with you," returned Modesty.

"I didn't expect you to be shamed with me, but you could have stayed with me after they left," replied Humility.

"I'm sorry. I was afraid of the Shame Enforcement Officers," said Modesty.

"Well, you have a good reason to be afraid; it was horrible," returned Humility. "It was the worst experience of my life. They stripped me naked and threw me into a dumpster. Inside it, I found some old men's clothing and this suitcase, which is full of books, not stones. I couldn't let go of it. They must have cursed me, because I dragged it all the way home without being able to get rid of it. I ran into some people on the street; they ridiculed me and spit on me."

"I am so sorry I wasn't there for you," said Modesty.

"Thank you," returned Humility. "I'm going to Spiritual Boulevard to see if I can find a place that will help me get rid of this suitcase. Do you want to go with me?"

"Sure," said Modesty.

Chapter Two

Looking for Answers

Not too far from her apartment was the popular Spiritual Boulevard, with its department stores, accessory shops, supply depots, emporiums, markets, offices, warehouses, meeting places, and restaurants. Each one of them specialized in specific spiritual services to the people of the city. Humility hoped to figure out what sort of spirituality would rid her of her burdensome Suitcase of Shame. The first place to catch her eye was the Religion Factory. It was several levels high and had a large neon sign on its roof. Neither she nor Modesty had visited Spiritual Boulevard before, and they both were caught off guard by its unfamiliar strangeness.

"What do you think about the Religion Factory?" suggested Humility. "Should we check it out first?"

"It's up to you. I think the Light and Darkness Café looks cool," returned Modesty.

"Alright, let's do that one next," said Humility.

"Works for me," replied Modesty.

"Searching for answers?" asked a young man who was leaning against a pole.

"Yes," returned Modesty.

"Me too," he replied. "My name is Courtesy. Would you like some help carrying that suitcase?"

"No, I got it," said Humility, but Courtesy grabbed it from her and swung it over his back.

"Wow, this is heavy. What's in here?" he said.

"What are you doing?" she returned. "That's my burden to carry."

"Is it?" he returned. "Well, then I'm going to help you carry it."

"You don't understand, I was shamed by the Shame Enforcement Officers, and the suitcase was my curse," said Humility. "And the only way I can get rid of the curse is by getting rid of the suitcase of shame."

"And how are you going to do that?" questioned Courtesy.

"I don't know, but I was hoping that by coming here I could figure it out," said Humility.

"I see, but nonetheless, there's no reason why I can't help you carry it," responded Courtesy. "Where are you going?"

"The Religion Factory," said Modesty.

"Alright," said Courtesy. "Lead the way."

"So, you're going with us?" asked Humility.

"Sure," said Courtesy, as the three of them walked, and Humility was glad to have help carrying the suitcase. When they got there, they were surprised that the only way into the building was a manhole sized opening in the concrete. It was a tall building, several levels high, and all its windows were blacked out with painted backgrounds and symbols of different religions. At the entrance of the hole was a little wooden sign that read, "The Religion Factory: down stairs." They went down the steps into the hole (with Courtesy wrestling with the suitcase) and met a receptionist at the bottom.

"Welcome to the Religion Factory," she said.

"What does a religion factory do?" asked Modesty.

"Many things," said the Receptionist. "We invent new religions. We expand old ones. We form new denominations. We also destroy religions, parts of them, and their denomination. We're a service company. We do it all for a fee."

"Who are some of your clients?" asked Humility.

"Oh, well, I can't give you their names, of course. We get religious groups, non-religious groups, individuals, and even city officials," said the Receptionist.

"They pay you to destroy religions?" asked Modesty.

"Yes, they do, and build them as well. Would you like to see? I can call someone to come and give you a tour, if you like," said the Receptionist.

"Okay," the three of them agreed.

After a few minutes, the shift Supervisor came through a door and greeted them. He gave them a brief introduction to the industry of religious construction and deconstruction, explaining to them that throughout thousands of years of history, religions formed and evolved by the natural selection of social events and outcomes of those events. However, in the past century, Religion Factories have reshaped the entire process. It all began with the invention of the Metaphysical Systematic Transformer (the MST), which is a technical way of saying that it can change entire systems of religious ideas.

"Wait, are you saying that this MST machine can actually change the way people think about religion?" asked Courtesy.

"Sort of," he responded. "It doesn't directly change the way people think, for that would be unethical, but rather it alters the concept of the religion in a new way that would be believable by the average citizen, and then uses social media and the word of mouth to change the way people think. I can give you guys a tour at three o'clock, which is in about two and a half hours, if you would like. Just come back then."

"We'll be here," said Courtesy.

"We will?" questioned Humility.

"Sure, why not?" suggested Modesty.

"I'll let you three figure it out," said the Supervisor.

They went back up the staircase (as Courtesy still carried the suitcase), and they headed for the Café of Light and Darkness. It was about a block away, on the other side of the street, and when they arrived they saw no tables to sit at. Instead, there were dozens of steel ladders that were bolted to the floor and ceiling (about twenty feet high) and extended out from each ladder was a large glass cylinder shaped transparent container, which was held up by the ladder and other steel poles connected to the ceiling. All around the café, people could be seen inside the containers, and also climbing up and down the ladders to get in and out of the containers. Then they saw a waitress climbing a ladder; while a tray of food was being lifted by a small elevator next to the ladder, and she stepped into the container where people were sitting and served them food.

At the container nearest to the entrance door, Humility, Modesty, and Courtesy watched as a waitress climbed up to the ladder and asked the people inside if they were ready for her to close the top. They said "yes," and then she asked them which one they wanted first, light or darkness. They said, "darkness first," and then she pushed a button on the side of the container, and instantly a metallic surface came inward from all sides of the circular container and closed at the center. The container was transparent glass, so they could be seen rather easily, but then suddenly it all went pitch black inside and the people were screaming shouts of fear and excitement.

"Welcome to the Light and Darkness Café. Chamber for three?" asked a waitress, as she came to the entrance to greet them.

"Sure," said Modesty. "But what is it?"

"This must be your first time," said the waitress.

"Yes," said Modesty.

"Great," said the waitress. "I'll explain it to you. You go up the ladder and climb down into the Light and Darkness Chamber and have a seat at the table inside it. Then you order food, we bring it to you, you eat, and after you're done we close the top and you experience both light and darkness in whichever order you prefer."

"Alright, yes, awesome," they told her with excitement.

They climbed up into a chamber in the back corner of the cafe, and each ordered the most exotic thing they could find on the menu, for it was already a strange experience, so they didn't want to ruin it by ordering something normal like a cheeseburger or pizza. Humility ordered the chocolate covered flying fish, stuffed with honey dipped baby frogs. Modesty had the fried carnivorous plant. Courtesy, who was so exhausted and hungry after spending so much energy getting the burdensome suitcase up the ladder, decided to order the largest thing on the menu; a smoked beehive.

When the food arrived, and as they were eating, Humility was shocked by how she felt and said, "You guys, do you feel something else besides what you normally feel when you eat really good food?"

"Yeah, but I never thought that this would even taste good, I just did it for the experience. But I do feel something else. What is it?" asked Modesty.

"I feel it too," said Courtesy. "And I know what you mean, Modesty, I never thought bees would be so good, and even the hive is amazing, but there is something else. I can't put my finger on it."

"I can't decide if it's bad or good," said Humility.

"It reminds me of the time that my dad and I found what we believed to be a hidden cave, and when we explored it, I was so afraid, but also excited," said Courtesy.

"Yeah, it reminds me of something like that too," said Humility. "It reminds me of the time I spied on my grandma, because I thought she was the serial killer I had heard about on the news, because she was always sneaking off somewhere."

"What, are you kidding me?" said Courtesy.

"No, but she wasn't the serial killer. It turns out the secret thing she was doing was attending a spiritual meeting, and she didn't want anyone else in the family to know," said Humility.

"I remember you telling me about that," said Modesty. "Do you remember what kind of meeting it was? Was it religious or more spiritually open?"

"I don't know," she returned. "Come to think of it, I may remember her saying something about the Bible.

"You should ask her," said Courtesy.

"She can't," said Modesty. "Her grandma died last year."

"Oh, I'm sorry," said Courtesy.

"Don't worry about it," said Humility, as the waitress came down into the chamber and took their plates.

"You guys ready?" she said.

"Excuse me, but do you know why the food makes us feel, sort of, mysterious?" questioned Courtesy.

"It's an effect from the way we cook our food," replied the waitress. "We use the same ingredients as everyone else, but we prepare it (using the right temperatures, sequences, and amounts), in such a way that it produces an effect in the food that stimulates the brain to release the feeling of mystery for the person who eats it."

"Why?" asked Humility.

"It's all a part of the show of Light and Darkness. You'll see," said the Waitress. "Are you ready?"

"I guess so," said Humility, and the others agreed. "Let's do the light first."

"You got it," said the Waitress, as she pushed the button to close the door.

The three of them instinctively held on to their chairs, and then suddenly the walls became solid white and no longer transparent, as the chamber filled with bright light and thousands of tiny bead sized spheres of intense light. They were everywhere, as if it was raining, but the raindrops stopped in mid-air, and just stayed there. Then Humility had the craziest idea. She wanted to put the little beads of light in her mouth. She wanted to eat them; to consume them. She grabbed one, between her thumb and pointer finger, and it wasn't hot, but it sent energetic sensations into her skin. She brought it closer to her face and opened her mouth.

"What are you doing," shouted Modesty, over the increasing sound of a pulsing noise. "You can't eat that."

"No, I think she's right," said Courtesy, as he grabbed a bead of light for himself.

"Modesty, I think we're supposed to eat them, like a dessert or something," said Humility, as she put the bead of light into her mouth and consumed it. The other two did the same and the feelings of intense satisfaction and joy was immediate for all three. They began grabbing every single bead of light and shoving them into their mouths, as if they were chocolate covered raisins. The suitcase suddenly caught their attention, because it was swelling with brightness.

"Look at the suitcase," said Humility.

"This container must have some kind of effect on the books, because they're glowing inside," said Courtesy.

"Let's open it," said Modesty, as she reached down and unlatched the suitcase, revealing a light so intense that their eyes could barely stay open. Then the light suddenly faded, from the books, and from everything else in the room.

"What's happening?" said Modesty.

"I think it's switching from light to darkness," said Humility. She was right, because the walls became transparent again, and they could see out into the rest of the café. However, it was only for a moment, because then the walls went totally black, light escaped from the container, and they could see nothing at all. They couldn't help but scream and shout with fear and excitement. Suddenly, they heard low murmurs all around them, like the painful groans of a dying man, and something in the dark was slightly pulling them from all directions.

"Something's grabbing me," screamed Modesty.

"Me too," shouted Humility.

"I think they are spirits or something," panicked Courtesy.

"Is this real or just part of the show," shouted Modesty.

"I don't know," returned Courtesy.

"It seems real," said Humility. "Look at the suitcase. My eyes are adjusting to the darkness, and I can see that something in there is still shining, although very faintly, it seems."

She bent down toward the suitcase, which was still open, and saw that one of the books was giving off a glowing light. However, she noticed that it wasn't because the light from the book was dim, but because something that looked like thick black smoke was smothering its light. She picked up the book, and thought she saw the words "Holy Bible" behind the thick black smoke like substance that was smothering it. She began to open the pages of the book, and what seemed to be a supernova of extreme light exploded outward, and instantly, the container was back to normal light, and the walls were transparent again.

The waitress saw them from the ground level, then climbed the ladder, opened the top and said, "Done all ready. That's odd, the darkness usually lasts longer. I wonder what happened."

"That's alright, I'm ready to go," said Humility, as she put the Bible back in the suitcase, closed it up, and began lugging it up the ladder inside the chamber, and then down the ladder on the outside, with a little help from the waitress. They paid for their meal and went out into the busy sidewalk of Spiritual Boulevard. They began walking slowly.

"Would you like me to carry the suitcase?" asked Courtesy.

"No thanks, it's mine to carry," returned Humility.

"Everything alright?" questioned Modesty. "You seem a little upset."

"No, I'm fine, I just want to get rid of this burden," she said.

"I know it's heavy and all, but it didn't seem to be much of a burden back inside that darkness," said Courtesy. "I mean, are we going to talk about what just happened?"

"What do you mean?" asked Modesty.

"That book Humility was holding stopped their machine. It actually vanquished the darkness, or something," said Courtesy.

"You might think that was good, but I don't," said Humility. "Did you see the way those people were looking at me; the ones who were waiting for a chamber to open up? The waitress too, she stared at me for a moment. The darkness went away, you could see through the walls again, and they saw me standing there with a Bible in my hands. It was so embarrassing. It was as if I was being shamed again. No, I don't care about what it did to the darkness; I just want to get rid of it."

"I don't think they knew it was a Bible you were holding," said Modesty. "I just think they were curious about us suddenly becoming visible, and you were holding a book. Yes, that was probably odd to them, but they didn't know it was a Bible."

"Look, I understand that you are burdened by those books, but you can't deny that in both the light session and the darkness session, those books were extraordinary. They interacted with the light and darkness chamber in a way that I don't think anyone expected."

"Fine," said Humility. "I admit it. The books are interesting, but they are still a burden of shame, and I want to get rid of them."

"Alright," said Courtesy. "Fair enough, let's try to find a spiritual wise man to help us."

"I see something up ahead," said Modesty. They got there and read the sign: Spiritual Wisdom. They went inside the small shop and saw a woman walking on the ceiling, and a man walking on the left wall. Both were walking with no apparent aid to keep them from falling, as if the laws of gravity did not apply to them.

"Excuse me, but how are you doing that?" asked Humility. Both the man and the woman came down and stood before them. The woman looked to be in her thirties and dressed in several layers of rainbow shaded tattered clothing; and the man, who was much older, was wearing patched quilted jeans and a black t-shirt.

"Welcome," the man said. "My name is Sophisticated, and this is my daughter, Sophia. We are seekers, keepers, and teachers of all the different sources of spiritual wisdom. You have just entered a very special place, you see. This room is an invention of my own. It demonstrates the relativity of truth."

"I am Courtesy, and this is Humility and Modesty. But I don't understand what you just said. Isn't there just one true answer to a question?" asked Courtesy.

"Oh, goodness, boy, of course not," replied Sophisticated.

"Should we give them a demonstration, Dad?" said Sophia.

"Yes, I think so," he replied, and then he turned to Humility, Modesty, and Courtesy, and pointed to the right wall. "Let me ask you something? Is that the wall or the floor?"

"The wall," responded Humility.

"Right you are," said Sophia, and then she stepped up onto the wall to the left of the entrance door, as if it was now underneath her, and gravity had changed from her point of view. Then the old man stepped onto the wall and waved for the others to follow. They did, and were shocked to find themselves standing on what was the wall, but was now underneath them. Everything had shifted from their perspective.

"Now let me ask you; is this the floor or the wall?" asked Sophisticated.

"It's still the wall, I think," said Humility, and she looked at her suitcase, which was still on the floor, and it was now sticking out from what seemed to be the wall on her right, but it was the floor a moment ago.

"Is it?" said Sophia. "Look at your suitcase, it still obeys gravity as if the floor is underneath it, but if you grabbed it and pulled it over here, it would join you in a different perspective of gravity."

"Then what we stand on now is the floor," said Modesty.

"It was the wall, but now it's the floor," said Courtesy.

"That's right," said Sophisticated. "Truth is relative, not absolute. There are many truths to one answer; many sources of wisdom. The right answer depends on one's perspective."

"They are really wise," said Modesty to Humility. "Ask them how to get rid of the suitcase. I bet they know how."

"What is in the suitcase?" asked Sophia.

"Some spiritual books, including a Bible," said Humility. "And I can't get rid of it."

"Oh, I see," said Sophisticated. "Well, that's because you haven't come to the realization that religions and their specific beliefs are relevant for those who believe them, but not relevant for those who don't believe them. All you have to do is stop believing the Bible is true, and then you will be able to get rid of it."

"But isn't the truth of the Bible relevant for all people," asked Courtesy. "I mean, doesn't the Bible and Christianity claim that it is the ultimate source of truth? Didn't Jesus say that he is the Truth?"

"Yes, he did say that, but he nor the Bible can be the ultimate truth, because there is no ultimate truth. I mean, not even gravity is ultimate. We have demonstrated that gravity is relative," said Sophia.

"Yes, that's right," laughed Sophisticated. "For example, this room that I have created would not let that suitcase change its gravitational perspective if the books inside it were universally true concepts. The reason is because the ideas are bonded to the physicality of the books in which hold them. Therefore, if the Bible was true for all, then you would not be able to bring it over here."

"Go ahead and grab it," said Sophia.

"Alright," said Humility.

"Wait," said Sophisticated. "Bring over something else, first, so you can see what we mean."

"I'll grab this chair," said Courtesy, as he brought the chair from the wall, and it fell to the floor in which they were standing, which used to be the wall, as if it too had changed its gravitational perception. Modesty grabbed a little table from the corner, and it changed its gravitation effect just like everything else. Humility found a glass jar and pulled it over as well.

"You see, the suitcase should come over to this wall, which is to us now the floor, just like the chair, table, and jar did," said Sophia.

Then something happened that seemed from the perspective of Humility, Modesty, and Courtesy, to be even stranger than what happened at the Light and Darkness Café. Humility went to grab the suitcase and it wouldn't budge. She pulled on it as she was lifting it up a staircase, and it moved, but it remained heavy and never hit the floor that they were standing on. She let go of the handle, and it fell to the wall, because what was to them a wall was obviously still the floor to the suitcase. Courtesy gave it a shot, then Modesty, and the same thing happened. The suitcase was acting as Sophisticated and Sophia said it would act if the books inside were universally true for all people.

"I don't believe it," said Sophisticated, as he grabbed the suitcase and dragged it all the way across the floor they were all standing on, and then he let it go.

Courtesy had stepped back over to the floor the suitcase was lifted from. He was now standing near the entrance door, and what he saw was four people standing on the wall to the left of the door, and one of them was lifting a suitcase all the way up to the ceiling. When Sophisticated dropped the suitcase, it fell from the ceiling and crashed open on the floor. They all came down to the floor in front of the door to observe the suitcase.

"I can't believe it," said Sophia.

"It's impossible," said Sophisticated.

"You broke the suitcase," said Humility. "How am I going to carry it now? All the books are going to fall out."

"I'll get some rope, so you can tie it shut," said Sophia.

"Thank you," said Humility.

"Does that mean that the Bible is true?" said Courtesy.

"I don't know," said Sophisticated. "This is blowing my mind."

"I found some strong rope that's easy to tie and untie," said Sophia, as she bent down and tied up the suitcase.

Sophisticated gave them a nervous look and said, "Why don't you guys go ahead and leave, because I don't want anything to do with those books."

The three of them departed and Courtesy checked his phone to see what time it was. "A quarter to three," he said. "Should we go back to the Religion Factory? Remember, the shift supervisor said he would give us a tour."

"I'm down," said Modesty. "Humility, what about you? Do you still want to go?"

"I guess," said Humility, who was becoming more discouraged by the moment, that she still had this burden of shame to carry.

"Let me carry that for a while," said Modesty, as Humility thanked her and handed it over, and the three of them crossed the street and went back toward the Religion Factory. "I think the Religion Factory should have some help for us, don't you?"

"I do," said Courtesy. And when they got there, they went down the stairs into the underground entrance and were met by the Supervisor.

"You made it," he said. "And a little early, that's good. Something came up, and I only have about fifteen minutes, which means we can only tour one of the religions. Each level focuses on specific religious types. For example, level five is Monotheism; level four is Pantheism; and three is Polytheism. Do you guys have a specific religion that you are curious about or want to know how it works?"

"What about Christianity?" asked Humility, because she had become more curious about the Bible.

"That's a good one. It's on the fifth level, Monotheism. Follow me to the elevator, and we'll head up there," said the Religion Factory Supervisor. When they got onto the elevator, he noticed the suitcase Modesty was dragging along. "What's with the suitcase? Do you have rocks in there? It looks heavy."

"It's actually mine. There are books inside, not rocks, but they're as burdensome as rocks," said Humility. "Modesty is helping me carry the load."

"That's nice of her," said the Religion Factory Supervisor, as he smiled at Modesty. "What kind of books?"

"Theology books," said Humility.

"Theology of the Bible?" asked the Religion Factory Supervisor.

"Yes, there's a Bible in there too," returned Humility.

"Are you a Christian?" he asked, and the elevator door opened into a huge factory room as large as a warehouse.

"No, I'm not, but I do want to know about it," said Humility.

"Well, that I can help you with. Here we are; the Monotheism level. Christianity is over to the right. Follow me," said the Religion Factory Supervisor. They followed him on a tour through the department of Christianity. It occupied about half of the long and wide warehouse floor, with Judaism and Islam occupying other areas. However, the Supervisor had only enough time to show them the department of Christianity. He first brought them to the manager's station.

"This is where it all begins," said the Religion Factory Supervisor, as he pointed to the manager's station. "This is the Manager of Christianity."

"Hello," he said to them, and they returned the greeting.

"At the beginning of his shift, the manager receives a list of task assignments from the administration department, and then he assigns them to different workers throughout the shift. Do you have anything you can show us?" asked the Religion Factory Supervisor.

"Sure do," replied the Manager of Christianity. "I've got a core change we can do right now."

"What's a core change?" asked Courtesy.

"We have three essential kinds of changes that we do to a religion," said the Manager of Christianity. "It could be an emotional change, which is when people feel differently about the religion. Another change we do is moral, which is when we change what the religion teaches about the virtue of knowing and doing right from wrong. And the third is what I'm about to do now, which is a core change. It's when we alter something major about the religion."

"Like what?" questioned Humility.

"For example, last year we changed what many Christian churches preached about Heaven. We received a very expensive order to take Heaven out of the Christian religion. This was a very difficult task, because Christianity is based upon the teaching of the Bible, and Heaven is a major theme throughout the Old and New Testaments," said the Manager of Christianity.

"That seems impossible, then," said Modesty.

"Difficult, yes, but not impossible," said the Manager of Christianity. "You see, all we have to do is make sure people don't read the places in the Bible where it speaks about Heaven. The best way to do that is to destroy the imaginative power of the Bible's descriptions of what Heaven is like."

"You would have to get your hands on all the Bibles in the world, and then take out all the descriptions about Heaven, but that I know is impossible, right?" asked Courtesy.

"Yes, that would be impossible," replied the Manager of Christianity. "But that's not what we do. We don't alter the actual words of the Bible, but instead alter the way people read them."

"Before you continue," said the Religion Factory Supervisor to the Manager of Christianity, "I have a meeting with a high profile Pantheistic client in a few minutes. Could I leave these three with you, and they can get a full tour of how this department works?".

"Not a problem at all, sir," said the Manager of Christianity.

"Thank you," he said, as he said goodbye.

"Now, where were we?" asked the Manager. "Oh, right, I was telling you that we can take something major out of a religion, without taking it out of their religious text. The way we do it is by getting them to ignore or devalue all the references to Heaven when they read the Bible, and then from there they begin to think about Heaven less and less in their life, until it is gone."

"I think I understand," said Humility. "The foundational structure of the religion (which in this case is Christianity), resides in the minds of the people, not in the religious text (which for Christianity is the Bible)."

"That's right," he returned. "We use something called an MST, which means, Metaphysical Systematic Transformer. It can't change physical things like words on a page, but it can change mental perceptions and concepts of those words. In other words, the MST causes people to recognize only certain aspects of something, not the totality of it."

"How do you get people to overlook Heaven?" asked Courtesy. "I'm not a Christian, but I've heard a little, and Heaven is always presented as a perfect place, with no pain or hatred. How could you get someone to ignore something as good as that?"

"Simple, we use shame," said the Manager of Christianity, and Humility suddenly became very uncomfortable. "The MST causes readers of the Bible to be ashamed of Heaven. If they're ashamed of Heaven, then they won't pay any attention to it when it comes up in the Bible or in other places."

"How do you get people to be ashamed of Heaven?" asked Modesty.

"Easy," he said. "It's all about association. The MST began by associating the desire for Heaven with escaping practical life and responsibilities. Then it associated imagining Heaven with images similar to fairytales, fantasy, and science fiction. It also associated thinking about Heaven as missing out on the life with God that people have now, in this life. What all three of these have in common is the belief that it is irresponsible, silly, and immature to think about things beyond this world."

"Did it work?" asked Humility.

"Of course," said the Manager of Christianity. "Heaven still appears to be a part of Christianity, but it isn't. If you asked a Christian if they believed in Heaven, they would certainly proclaim yes, but only because they believe saying no would be a sin. In reality, in the past year, Heaven has almost completely departed from religious discussion between Christians. We've conducted internet analysis reports, which reveal that only less than 1% of Sunday sermons are about Heaven, and less than 1% of people who identify as Christians in social media mention Heaven or eternal life in their posts."

"What was it before?" asked Modesty.

"We brought it down from about 60% in church sermons, and down from 20% in social media."

"I'm not sure what to think about it all," said Humility.

"We get that a lot," said the Manager of Christianity. "It's alright; let me show you what we're doing today. We have an order from a large church here in the City of Spirituality. The subject is prayer, and it looks like they want Christianity to be known as people who pray more than any other religion, and more important than any other spiritual discipline. Follow me, and I'll show you how it's done."

The Manager of Christianity led them into the research room. He sat down at a desk and entered data into a computer that looked more like the panel of a music producer, with its hundreds of lights, labels, switches, nobs, levers, and sliding controls. Then a thick plastic card came out of a thin slit in the computer panel, about the size of a debit card, and he grabbed a hold of it.

"What's that?" asked Courtesy.

"This is the research card," replied the Manager of Christianity. "We update this computer everyday with every amount of religious information possible. When I put the information from the order into the computer, it then did a systematic research analysis regarding the task assignment. In this case, it would have formulated different definitions of prayer from the Bible, theology books, church sermons, and social media. A single subject like prayer may have as many as 10,000 definitions."

"10,000?" questioned Humility. "How could there be so many definitions of one word?"

"It surprises you, I see. Well, that's what's out there. The computer forms only as many definitions as there are in current culture," said the Manager of Christianity. "Now we take it to the MST, which is in the room next to this one, and it will use all 10,000 definitions of Christian prayer to change the way people perceive it."

They went into the MST room, and the Manager of Christianity put the plastic card into a card slot reader in a wall computer, with its panel of nobs and switches spread across the entire back wall. A moment later, the card ejected, and he grabbed it, while explaining that the MST just changed Christianity to be more focused on prayer.

"Just like that?" asked Modesty.

"Just like that," he repeated back to her.

"What does MST stand for again?" asked Courtesy.

"Metaphysical Systematic Transformer, which means that it can change the way people think about religion."

"You just changed the way we think about Christian prayer?" question Humility.

"Not yet, first we changed it in metaphysical reality, and then I will bring it to a third room, where it will then be implemented in the culture," said the Manager of Christianity, as he took them to a room filled with people sitting in front of computer screens on social media websites. They were posting, blogging, messaging, building ads, and creating new groups and pages. They took a closer look, and he explained to them that each person was conducting a different task.

"Listen up everyone, I'm putting your current assignments on hold and starting a new assignment," said the Manager of Christianity, as he slid the card into a small card reader at the table everyone was sitting at. The table circled along the four walls of the room, holding 30 computers, 30 chairs, and 30 people. All of their computer screens suddenly lit up with information on the new assignment.

"I'm sorry, but I suddenly don't feel too good," panicked Humility. "Could you show me the way out?"

"Yes, right this way," said the Manager of Christianity.

"We'll go with her," said Modesty, and Courtesy agreed.

"Let me have my suitcase," said Humility, as she grabbed it from Modesty.

When they got outside to the sidewalk on Spiritual Boulevard, Humility had gone into a full panic attack. She sat on her suitcase, grabbing fistfuls of her own hair, rocking back and forth, and muttering the words, "I don't know… I don't know… I don't know…" in a way that caused people to look at her with confusion, concern for her health, and even in amusement.

"Are you okay?" asked Courtesy.

"Yes, fine," said Humility, as she stood up

"I thought it was interesting," said Courtesy.

"Yeah, it's real interesting that people are telling us what to think," said Humility.

"It's just religion; just social media," responded Courtesy. "Those things don't really matter."

"I want to come to my own conclusion about what I believe," said Humility. "Those people are controlling us all like puppets. Or more accurately, it's their clients who are the puppet masters."

"I didn't know you felt so strongly about it," said Courtesy.

"Neither did I," said Modesty. "But I will admit that something seemed rather suspect about their whole program. I mean, they said that machine, the MST I think he called it, could change the metaphysics of a religion, but I don't think that's what was really going on."

"Do you think it was really all about social media?" asked Humility.

"That's exactly what I think," said Modesty. "That company claims to be able to change religions, but all I think they can do is use social media to influence people to think differently about religion."

"Well, they seem to be successful at that much at least," said Courtesy. "I mean, that manager guy said that they were able to actually get churches to preach less on certain topics by simply using social media."

"Do you think he was right, then, that if you change the way people think about religion, then you change the religion?" asked Modesty.

"I don't know," said Humility. "Well, I've had enough of this place for one day. I'm going home."

"Are you walking or taking the bus?" asked Modesty.

"The bus, I guess," said Humility.

"I'll go with you," said Modesty.

"I have a car," said Courtesy. "I can give you both a ride home."

"Sure, thank you," they both replied, and that was the end of spiritual Boulevard.

Chapter Three

Something to be Ashamed of

On Sunday Morning, Humility didn't go to church. She didn't read the Bible, pray, sing songs about God, or even think about God what so ever. In fact, you can't do any of those things when you're sleeping. The first time she looked at the clock was at 11:00 a.m., and after she closed her eyes for a little while longer, she looked again and saw that it was noon. She finally got out of bed at 1:00 p.m. She couldn't remember the last time she had slept for so long. She tried to remember what time she went to bed and thought that it was no later than 8:00 p.m.

With a bowl of cereal, she sunk into her couch and turned on the TV. Flipping through the channels, she was appalled at how many offered her nothing at all to watch, but then she finally settled on the coverage of a local event. The reporter was interviewing people at the 10th annual South East 32nd Avenue Spiritual Block party held at the Righteous Walker Memorial Park. Humility nearly choked on a cheerio when she heard this, because she moved into her apartment only six months earlier and had no idea that an annual spiritual block party was held just outside. She went to the window, opened the curtains, and there it was, a massive amount of people jammed into the park and experiencing spiritual booths of food, merchandise, and events.

Suddenly, there was a knock at the door, and Modesty's voice, "Hey it's me, open up."

"Hey," said Humility, as she opened the door and let her best friend in.

"Did you just wake up?" asked Modesty.

"Yeah, so what," said Humility.

"Honestly, Humility, there's an amazing world out there, full of great adventures, and wonderful people to meet, and you're going to miss out if you stay in here all day," said Modesty.

"What are you so cheerful about?" questioned Humility.

"A graveyard would seem cheerful compared to you right now," she returned.

"Thanks," replied Humility.

"I get it, you're down about yesterday, but it wasn't all a waste of time," said Modesty.

"What do you mean?" said Humility.

"Well, after Courtesy and I dropped you off yesterday, he took me home, but before I got out of the car we got to talking and we sort of hit it off. I gave him my number, and this morning he called me to ask if I would like to go with him to a spiritual block party. I said yes, and didn't realize until now that it was right next to your apartment," said Modesty.

"You're going on a date with him?" asked Humility.

"Yeah, what do you think?" asked Modesty.

"He seems like a good fit for you," returned Humility.

"Really, I'm glad you think so," said Modesty.

"Where is he?" asked Humility.

"We're meeting down there at two. Are you coming?" said Modesty.

"Sure, but I don't want to crowd in on your date. Besides, I'm going to see if I can get some help with my wonderful suitcase," said Humility.

"No, please, Humility, I want you to come along. It will make it less weird if you're there, and I want to be there with you to get rid of the suitcase," said Modesty.

"What? Are you scared or something?" questioned Humility.

"Terrified," said Modesty.

"Alright, I'll stay with you. At least for a little while," said Humility.

"No, you can't. Promise me you won't leave," said Modesty.

"Alright, calm down," she returned.

Humility got ready, while Modesty looked out the window, and at 2:00 p.m. they went down and met Courtesy outside at the park entrance into the Spiritual Block Party. There were thousands of people. Some were sitting and eating; some were walking from booth to booth; some were grouped in conversations; and others were taking part in activities. Humility caught a few looks from people who saw her dragging her burdensome suitcase, but she tried to ignore them.

She looked at everything that was going on and wondered where they might go first. She saw signs that read: Mind Reader; Fortune Teller; Healer; Signs and Wonders; Magical Books; Prophecy; Miraculous Objects; Find Your Spirituality; Wisdom of Many Colors; Embrace Your Darker Side; Forgiveness; Pick a Religion; the Truth; the Real Truth; the Ultimate Truth; the Factual Truth; Your Truth; the Old Truth; the New Truth; and Truth is Dead.

"What do you think?" asked Modesty.

"I don't know. What do you think?" he returned.

"I don't know either. What looks appealing to you guys," said Humility.

"It looks like a lot of people are gathering to see Miraculous Objects," said Courtesy.

"I don't know if we can even get close to that one," said Modesty. "I think anything about truth looks good."

"What about Truth is Dead?" asked Humility.

"Sure," said both Modesty and Courtesy at the same time, and they looked at each other with a smile.

"Although, Find Your Spirituality, seems relevant," said Humility.

"True," said Courtesy.

"Why don't you go to a Christian booth?" asked Courtesy. "It might be able to help you."

"Maybe, but all Christianity has done so far is provide the weight for my heavy shame," said Humility.

"Let's go to, Truth is Dead, first, then, Find Your Spirituality, and then, Forgiveness," said Modesty.

"Sounds good," said Courtesy.

"I think that will work," said Humility.

When the three of them got through the crowd to the, Truth is Dead booth, they realized that it wasn't a booth but a tent. They went inside and saw only three small children playing with wooden blocks at a little table in the center. A few people followed in after them, but soon left when they realized that it was just a tent with some kids playing. Courtesy was most intrigued with the mystery of the whole thing. He wondered if these kids were a part of the demonstration that truth is dead.

"Excuse me," he said. "We came for the, Truth is Dead exhibit."

"Do you really believe that truth can die?" said a woman who suddenly came through a slit in the tent that was the doorway between two tents.

"I don't know. I suppose not," said Courtesy.

"What about you girls?" she asked.

"If truth is reality, then how can it die?" questioned Modesty.

"Ah, but is truth reality, or is it perception?" asked the woman, as she sat down at the table to play with the kids.

"Perception," said Humility.

"Right," said the woman. "What's your name, honey?"

"Humility," she replied.

"Well, Humility, let me ask you, are these children truly children, or is that just your perception?" said the Woman, as Humility took a closer look and realized they were just puppets.

"Oh, whoa, but they seemed so real," said Humility.

"Yes, and I bet you thought I was a woman," she replied, as she took off her wig, wiped off her make-up, and took off her dress, revealing a t-shirt and jeans beneath.

"You're a man," said Courtesy.

"I am, but more importantly than my gender, I think, is whether this room we are in is in a tent or in a steel box?" he said. "Go ahead and check."

"I will," said Humility, as she touched the fabric of the tent wall, but felt nothing until her hand reached the hard steel behind the fabric. Then the man pulled a little controller out of his pocket and pushed a button. Instantly, the sight of the tent disappeared, and all they saw was the inside of a large steel container, like the one on a ship or train. The door of the container was open, but they could tell that the outside appearance of the tent was still deceiving everyone on the outside.

"So, the outside of the tent is also just a projection?" asked Humility.

"That's right," she said. "People look at it and think they are seeing a tent, but they are really seeing a steel box."

"Is this what you mean by saying that truth is dead; that things may not be what they seem to be, which makes them untrue, and since we never know if something truly is what it seems to be, then truth is dead?" asked Courtesy.

"That's right," said the man. "Please, call me Postmodernism. I must admit that the title of, Truth is Dead, is a little dramatic, but it is catchy, and for that reason it brought you here, so I do not apologize. However, it's not that truth is dead, but that truth is invisible. It's like the wind, you see. Sure, we can see that it's there when it moves things, but who can catch it? And if someone did catch it, there would be no way to prove that he did, because what he caught would be invisible."

"You might be just the person I'm looking for," said Humility.

"Really, why is that?" asked Postmodernism.

"It's this suitcase," she replied. "Inside it is a Bible and theology books, which burden me with shame."

"Shame, you say," said Postmodernism. "I should wonder if it is necessary. Maybe you can just set that suitcase on fire and be done with it. Here, I have some matches and lighter fluid. We'll do it right here and now if you want."

"I don't know," said Humility. "I'm not certain I want to do that. I still have questions."

"Ask away," said Postmodernism.

"Is the Bible true?" she asked.

"There's no way to know for sure," said Postmodernism.

"Then I shouldn't burn it, because it might be true," said Humility.

"Yes, but you'll never be able to know, so why carry the burden of something that might not be true?" said Postmodernism.

"It would be worth it if the Bible was true," said Humility.

"You'll never know if it is true," said Postmodernism.

"Maybe some things can be proven to be true," said Humility.

"Like what?" asked Postmodernism.

"Like mathematics," said Humility. "In the same way that mathematics proves to be true, maybe there's a way to prove that God and the Bible is true."

"I think you're missing the point," said Postmodernism. "Mathematics can prove physical laws but cannot prove metaphysical laws. That is, there is no place for math when dealing with ideas and concepts like justice, love, and goodness. Those kinds of things are based upon the perception of the individual, which means there are many true answers to what is just, loving, and good; as many as there are people to perceive them."

"You're saying that there is no one set of rules or laws that we should all measure ourselves against," said Courtesy.

"That's exactly what I'm saying," said Postmodernism. "We are free to live to our own convictions. Treat others the way you would like to be treated. Isn't that what Jesus said?"

"Yes, I believe he did say that, but didn't he also say that anyone who does not do what he says is a fool," said Courtesy.

"And that's why I'm not a Christian," said Postmodernism. "Christians say that if you don't believe what they believe then you're a fool. That's so egotistical."

"I agree," said Courtesy.

"Me too," said Modesty.

"Good," said Postmodernism, as he turned to Humility. "What about you?"

"I don't know," she responded. "I mean, yes, that would be messed up if a person called you a fool if you didn't believe everything he believed, and if you didn't do everything he wanted you to do. However, I'm not an expert, but didn't Jesus claim to be the Creator of the Universe? Doesn't that give him the authority to say what he did?"

"Are you a Christian, young lady?" asked Postmodernism.

"No, but I want to know the truth," she replied.

"Well, as I've already told you, that kind of truth is impossible to know. However, you both are on the right track," he said to Modesty and Courtesy. But to Humility he said, "If you ever choose to give up your pursuit of the truth, you will be on the right track too. Good day to you."

"Thank you," said Modesty, as the three of them went back outside to the Spiritual Block Party.

"What a hypocrite," said Humility.

"Really?" asked Modesty. "I thought he was interesting."

"Yeah, he made some good points," said Courtesy, as they stood surrounded in the park by hundreds of people.

"He said that if I chose to give up my pursuit of the truth that I will be on the right track," said Humility.

"Yeah, so, how is that hypocritical?" asked Modesty.

"What he means by the right track, he means the true one, and yet he wants me to give up my pursuit of truth. However, if I did that, then why would I ever follow his so called right track? If you ask me, I think he wants us to believe that truth can't be discovered, simply so that we will believe that what he says is true."

"I see what you mean," said Courtesy. "Even his statement, that truth cannot be found, is a statement of truth. He wants us to believe it, yet, it's a contradiction of itself."

"Right," said Modesty. "He's basically saying, 'the truth is, that there is no truth.'"

"And if there is no truth, then the statement itself cannot be true," said Courtesy.

"So, it's impossible to say that truth cannot be found, because it would disqualify the very statement you're making," said Modesty.

"Right," said Courtesy.

"You guys are geniuses," said Humility.

"Thanks," they both responded at once.

"Do you know what this means?" said Humility.

"What does it mean?" asked Modesty.

"It means that the existence of truth is self-evident, like mathematics," said Courtesy.

"That's right," said Humility. "This means that our pursuit of truth is not in vain."

"Just because the existence of truth itself is self-evident, that doesn't mean we can find it," said Modesty. "For example, we can see stars that are millions of miles away, but we cannot get to them. Maybe knowing whether the Bible is true is kind of like that. In other words, knowing the possibility that the Bible is true is like seeing the stars, but knowing certainly that it is true would be like traveling to a star and seeing it up-close."

"Brilliant," said Courtesy.

"Thank you," returned Modesty.

"Yes, I agree," said Humility.

"Where should we go next?" said Modesty.

"Find Your Spirituality," said Courtesy.

"Alright, let's go," said Humility.

They came to a large crowd of people encircled around a spiritual wise man with a portable microphone/speaker (or a bullhorn), like the one a police officer uses. The man walked around a young woman sitting on a tall wooden stool in the center of the circle. The man was asking the woman questions about her spirituality. After a few minutes, he declared that her spirituality was the rabbit. Then he invited a man from the crowd to sit on the stool, and a few minutes later he declared him an elk. And it went on like this for a half hour. An older woman was a salmon; a teenage girl a bobcat; a young man a garden snake; and an older man a bear. Then the man was pointing to Courtesy to come sit on the chair.

He sat down and answered all the bazar questions the man asked him. In what kind of way would he prefer to die? What is the first color he remembers from his childhood? Would he rather eat a pile of sand or a pile of dust? Is he more comfortable up really high or in a tight enclosed space? How many people does he know that are afraid of the darkness? What city was he born? Does he prefer red meat or white meat? Can he sit in a place for a long time without moving? Can he roam for a long time without having to stop? He declared Courtesy to have the spirituality of a humpback whale. Then Courtesy briefly told the man about Humility's suitcase problem, and that she wanted to know her spirituality.

"Very well then, let's have her up here," he said, looking at her. "Come on over and have a seat, young lady. And what do we have here?"

"It's something I need to get rid of," said Humility, talking about her suitcase of shame. "I got it out of the dumpster."

"I see, well, maybe you should put it back where you got it," said the Spiritual Wise Man.

"I would if I could, but I can't," said Humility.

"Oh, well, I'm sorry to hear that," he said, but he wasn't sorry, because he knew how she got the suitcase. "Tell me, what's in the suitcase?"

"A Bible and other theology books," she replied.

"Are you a Christian?" he asked.

"No," she said.

"So, you want to get rid of this burden, then?" he questioned.

"Yes," she affirmed.

"Well, I know your spirituality, young lady," said the Spiritual Wise Man. "You're a maggot, and soon you'll transform into a fly. You see, you feed on garbage, like the trash you carry with you in that suitcase. But you can't get rid of it, because it's who you are. You can't help to be shamed by it, because you're a filthy maggot. That's reality, and there's nothing you or I can do about it."

"I'm a maggot?" questioned Humility, who had turned as red as a radish.

"That's right, young lady," he returned, as he signaled to someone in the crowd to go and get the Shame Enforcement Officers, because he knew Humility was about to disagree with him.

"Why would you say that to me?" questioned Humility.

"Don't get me wrong," he explained, making sure that it was clear he was talking about spirituality, so that the Shame Enforcement Officers would get involved. "It's not your character as a person I'm referring to, but your spirituality. It's obvious that in a spiritual sense, you'll never rise above spiritual garbage, because maggots and flies never do; it's just the way it is."

"I'm not a spiritual maggot," replied Humility.

"Really; is that so? Then, you disagree with me?" he said.

"As a matter of fact, I do," she declared.

"Humility, no, don't do it," shouted Modesty, as she and Courtesy came out into the center of the crowd of people and attempted to drag Humility away.

"No, let go," she said to them, and then she spoke to the crowd about the Spiritual Wise Man. "I don't care if I am shamed again. This man thinks he is spiritually wise, but he is a fool. I have already told you that I am not a Christian, but I know the Bible is not garbage. I am not a maggot."

"What's going on here?" said a Shame Enforcement Officer. "Girl, I heard that you called that man a spiritual fool. How dare you break the law right here in front of all these people? I remember you from Friday, when we shamed you for doing the same thing. Why couldn't you learn your lesson?"

"It's from those books you cursed her with," said a girl. Humility looked around to see who spoke and was horrified to see that it was Modesty.

"What books?" asked one of the Shame Enforcement Officers.

"When you threw her into the dumpster, she came out with a suitcase, which you cursed her to carry with her. Can't you see? That suitcase caused her to become spiritually rebellious. Understand? It's your fault."

"I see what you mean," said the Shame Enforcement Officer, who was accompanied by two other officers. We can take care of that."

"Don't touch me," screamed Humility, as the Shame Enforcement Officers grabbed her, and the entire population of the Spiritual Block Party was now watching from within huge crowds of people throughout the park. They threw her onto the ground, gagged her mouth, tied her hands and feet, and bound a chain from her neck to the suitcase. Then they smothered the suitcase with so many chains and locks that no one could see the surface of it.

"There we go," pronounced the Shame Enforcement Officer to all the people watching, "We have cursed it again, so that she cannot get rid of it. This time, the curse will allow no one to help her carry the burden, and she will have to drag it by her neck, without the aid of her hands. We will release the gag, and the binding on her hands and feet, but no one is to help her, speak to her, or make contact with her in any way whatsoever. Is that understood? If anyone here breaks my command, they will be treated as equally guilty."

Humility screamed for a while, but eventually realized the pointlessness of it. The crowd remained there, silent, and unresponsive to her. They cleared a path for her to drag her suitcase out by her neck. She screamed and cursed everyone there, including her former friends, who in her mind had betrayed her. Her apartment was right next to the park, and so the walk wasn't that far. Three Shame Enforcement Officers followed her to the apartment building, up the stairs, and through the hall, making sure that no one helped her. She opened her door, went in, closed it, and they went back to their patrol obligations.

Humility fell to the floor, and all she did was cry. It wasn't until hours later that she could think even a single positive thought. They slowly came into her mind. First, she realized that not everyone agreed with the laws of the City of Spirituality, and they just went along for fear of being punished. Then she thought that wishing they were all cursed was unfair, because it was really the City of Spirituality that is to blame for creating such laws that would shame women for spiritual authority.

"I wish God was real," she admitted, speaking it out loud to herself. "But there's no way to know for sure."

"The Word of God is with you," came suddenly into her mind, just like before. It was a thought, but not her own; she could tell. She decided to speak to the thoughts.

"Are you someone else; not me?" she questioned.

"I am the Word of God," said the voice in her thoughts.

"Do you mean the Bible?" she asked.

"The Bible is my words, but I am not the Bible. It is just a book, but its words are mine. I am the word of God," said the voice in her thoughts.

"Are you saying that you are God?" asked Humility.

"That's right," said the Word of God. "I'm glad you finally figured out what the phrase 'the Word of God' means."

"What do you want me to do?" she asked.

"I want you to have hope," replied the Word of God.

"How am I supposed to have hope?" she asked.

"I am going to give it to you," he replied.

"Does this mean that I have to become a Christian?" asked Humility.

"No, it doesn't," he said. "I only want you to be able to do what it is that you have set out to do. I want you to be able to seek out your true spirituality, and I hope that you will find it."

"Thank you," she said.

"You are welcome," replied the Word of God, and then the chains on the suitcase shattered into thousands of pieces, and Humility's neck was now free from it.

"Are you still there?" asked Humility.

"Yes," he replied.

"Will you tell me how to get rid of my burden of shame?" she asked.

"Yes, I will. Go to the church on the other side of town; on the corner between Propitiation Street and Expiation Street. There you will find a pastor who will guide you and answer all your questions," said the Word of God.

"I thought you said I didn't have to become a Christian," said Humility.

"Yes, that is still true. I am only sending you to the best place to get rid of your burden. If you don't like it, you can just leave. Why don't you read from my book?" he said.

"Alright," said Humility.

She opened the Bible and read, "Fear not, for you will not be ashamed; be not confounded, for you will not be disgraced; for you will forget the shame of your youth."

She was so overwhelmed by the pleasure and hope of this message that she shouted in gladness, cried in joy, and began to believe that maybe the voice she perceived in her thoughts was real. She became very excited about the chance that she might be able to get rid of her burden of shame.

Chapter Four

Willing to Die

An older Asian woman named Shy was sitting on a large city transit max train, with her traveling bag between her legs, reading a book of spirituality, and keeping to herself. She was a very experienced bus rider. After 30 years of commuting to work, she knew as well as anyone how to keep safe. Nearly every day, something illegal or suspicious was taking place between max stops, but Shy ignored it the best she could.

When suddenly, there were a group of people shouting at a girl, Shy took no notice of it. But then, the last thing she ever wanted or expected, happened. The girl they were shouting at sat down in the empty seat next to her. How unfortunate. She began to fill up with sorrow. She tried to ignore it, but she couldn't; it was too close to her. Right next to her, in fact; only inches away.

Shy looked over and observed a young woman, and in her grasp was a tattered suitcase. Standing around her and towering over both of them were a group of ridiculers. She learned from what they were saying to the girl with the suitcase, that they had seen her a few days earlier, and she was shamed by the Shame Enforcement Officers.

Of course, as the reader already knows, the girl, Humility, is on her way across town to a Christian church to seek answers about how to get rid of her burdensome suitcase. This was not her idea, but the idea of a thought-like voice that had internally spoken to her. Then, while this was taking place, another ridiculer joined the group and told everyone how he had witnessed this girl get shamed as a spiritual block party, and then everyone realized that Humility had been shamed twice.

"This little rat can't learn her lessons," said the Ridiculer's Girlfriend.

"I don't want any trouble," returned Humility.

"Shut your mouth, or I will shut it for you," shouted the Ridiculer's Girlfriend, as her boyfriend grabbed her wrist and held her back from hitting Humility.

"Not here, Darling," said the Ridiculer. "We can follow her off the max and get her when no one is watching."

"What have I done to you?" pleaded Humility. "Why can't you just leave me alone?"

"You're a disease, and we can't have you infecting anyone else," said the Ridiculer.

The train was coming to a stop, and suddenly the little Asian woman named Shy reached into her bag and pulled out a can of pepper-spray. The ridiculers didn't know what hit them. Everyone on the bus, including Shy, were shocked by the screams the pepper spray produced from its victims. However, it was too late, the damage was already done. Shy was horrified. A dozen people were on the bus floor screaming and squirming like tortured insects.

The problem is that Shy had never used pepper-spray before and had no idea how much pain it caused. It had been over twenty years since she had experienced any sort of confrontation with a person, and naturally, her fear of it made her over compensate the amount of pepper-spray she used. It caught the ridiculers by surprise. No one had even noticed her sitting there. Shy rose to her feet, aimed the can at the Ridiculer, and sprayed until he dropped. Two seconds later, she turned to his girlfriend and sprayed until she dropped. She did the same to every person who was standing over her and Humility.

It took only thirty seconds to pepper spray 5 ridiculers. The train had come to a stop, and Shy was sobbing, "I'm sorry," to all her victims.

"We have to leave," sobbed Humility, who had also become emotional by the screaming and seemingly tortured people all squirming on the floor. They got off the max train, and others followed, even if it wasn't their stop, because the fumes from the pepper spray had left a cloud in the air that caused immediate coughing and burning skin. In fact, Humility soon realized that her tears were not from being sorry, but from her burning eyes.

After the girls hurried and walked a few blocks away, Humility introduced herself. "Who are you, and why did you help me?"

"I'm Shy. I did it because I was afraid they were going to do something awful to you," she said.

"I think they would have, so thank you," said Humility.

"Are they going to be okay?" asked Shy.

"I don't know, but they will learn a good lesson, I think," said Humility.

"Yeah, don't mess with people, because you never know if someone has a can of pepper-spray," said Shy.

"You sure shocked them," said Humility. "They didn't even notice you were there; then you blasted them. They didn't see it coming, and by the time they could have fought back, they were down on their faces, screaming in agony."

"Where are you going?" asked Shy.

"There is a church on this side of town that I'm trying to get to. It's on the corner Expiation and Propitiation street. Do you know where that is?" questioned Humility.

"Yeah, I do. It's called the Church of Atonement. I've never been there, but I've walked past it before," said Shy. "You know, it's not actually on the corner of those streets. It's at the center of them. They are both the same street. One street goes around the church property, like a circle. If you go one direction, the street sign says, Expiation, and if you go the other direction, the street sign says, Propitiation."

"Weird," said Humility. "What do those words mean?"

"I have no idea," said Shy.

"How do I get there from here?" asked Humility.

"Easy," said Shy. "This road that we are on is Perfection Road, just go that way, and you will run right into it after about a mile or so."

"Alright, thanks. Where are you going?" said Humility.

"Home, which is the opposite direction. Can I ask what you are going to a church for?" said Shy. "Those ridiculers said something about you having a Bible in that suitcase. Are you a Christian?"

"It's a long story, and no, I am not a Christian. I am going to the church to get answers as to how I can get rid of this burdensome suitcase," said Humility.

"Oh, I see. Well, good luck," she said, as they said goodbye and set out in different directions.

Humility dragged her burdensome suitcase of shame down Perfection Road toward the Church of Atonement. It was so heavy. She tried to keep it off the ground, but she wasn't successful. It dragged on the concrete sidewalk, making a sound that could be heard by the on-looking people in the houses on each side of the street, and the rope that held it together from the Light and Darkness Café was coming undone.

Suddenly, the suitcase of burdensome shame broke open, and the books spilled out onto the sidewalk. This caused Humility to lose control. She kicked the suitcase and stomped on it with the entire weight of her body. Then she picked up one of the smaller theology books and threw it as high and far as she could. It brought her enormous relief, and surprised her, because she thought she couldn't get rid of the books. Maybe she could just throw them all away. Then she was shocked to see that the book she threw didn't fall to the ground, but changed its course back toward her, and flew right back to her, like a boomerang. It hit her square in the chest and knocked her down.

"Are you okay?" said a woman coming out of her house. "That book hit you hard, but I don't have a clue how it was possible. Wasn't that the book you threw?"

"I'm alright," said Humility. "These books are cursed. I was shamed by the Shame Enforcement Officers."

"Oh dear, I can't help you, then," said the Woman. "If you were shamed, then you got what you deserve."

"I need some tape to bind my suitcase, or I'll never make it to the church," said Humility.

"I don't have any," said the Woman.

"Can you at least give me a ride?" asked Humility.

"I can't help you," said the Woman.

"What am I supposed to do?" shouted Humility, and at this point she was speaking not only to the woman, but also to the people staring at her from their windows and porches.

"Not my problem," shouted the woman.

"But I'm stuck," returned Humility.

"You shouldn't have gone and gotten yourself shamed, then," shouted the woman, before she went into her house.

"Great," said Humility. "How am I supposed to get anywhere with this God-forsaken broken suitcase?"

However, as she looked down the road toward the church, which she could see about a quarter of a mile away, she saw a man walking toward her. He was waving his hands and appeared to be trying to get her attention. When he got closer, she saw him holding up a roll of duct-tape in his right hand."

"How did you know I needed help?" said Humility, as the man approached her.

"God told me," he said.

"Who are you?" asked Humility.

"I'm Pastor Guidance, of the Church of Atonement, just down the road," he said, as he knelt down and began binding up the hole in the suitcase with his roll of tape.

"Seriously, how did know I am here, and that I needed tape?" questioned Humility.

"God told me," he returned. "He told me this morning that you were coming to seek guidance about how to get rid of your burden, and just a few minutes ago he told me that you were here, but that you needed help with binding your suitcase; I grabbed some tape and began walking."

"So, you're the one who is supposed to help me get rid of this burden," said Humility. "Well, why can't you tell me how to get rid of it now, and I can be done with it right here and now."

"We have to take it back to the church to get rid of it. We can't do it here," said Pastor Guidance. "Here, it looks heavy; let me help you carry it."

Humility accepted his offer, and the two of them carried her broken suitcase of theology books a quarter mile to the church. Along the way, she thought about how kind it was that this man had come to her aid and helped her. She was puzzled, though. How could this all be just a coincidence? A voice in her thoughts told her to come to a place that she never knew about, and it was really there. This pastor happened to come to her aid at just the right moment. He claimed that God told him to do it. Could God be real?

When they arrived at the church, Pastor Guidance showed Humility to his office. It was a room about the size of a bedroom, with books from floor to ceiling on every wall, and a desk in the center with a chair on each side. The two of them had a seat at the desk and took a moment of silence. It seemed that the Pastor was giving Humility the opportunity to speak first, and out of respect, she was giving him the right to speak first. It was an awkward two minutes before Humility spoke.

"So, is it true that you can help me get rid of my burden, or do I have to become a Christian, first?" she said.

"Do you want to be a Christian?" he returned.

"No."

"Why not?"

"That's not why I came here," she said.

"I see, you just want to get rid of your burdensome suitcase of shame," he said.

"Yes, but I don't see why I should have to be religious to be free of this burden," said Humility. "If I wanted to be religious, then I would just keep the suitcase."

"What makes you say that?" asked Pastor Guidance.

"Well, it's full of religious books, isn't it?" she replied. "Besides, everything that I know about religion seems to be just as burdensome and shameful as carrying this suitcase around. That's why I was reluctant to come to a church for help. It seems that Christianity would add to my burden, not take it away."

"If that was true, then where is your burdensome suitcase of shame?" he said, as Humility looked down beside her chair and saw that it was not there. She quickly got up and searched all around the office and didn't see it.

"Where is it?" she questioned.

"Why, do you want it back? I thought you wanted to get rid of it," he returned.

"I do, but did you really get rid of it?" said Humility.

"Not completely, because the moment you leave this church, your burden will come back," he said.

"Then, it's not really gone," said Humility.

"Let me ask you a question," said Pastor Guidance. "Since you first received your burden, have you been able to do anything without it?"

"No, except sleep, but even in my dreams I am carrying that dreadful suitcase," she said.

"What is something that you have wanted to do, that you couldn't do with that suitcase?" he asked.

"The suitcase is a nightmare for anything I do," said Humility.

"We have a large garden on the church property, which means you can walk without your burden. Why don't we go for a walk, and you can see for yourself that the suitcase is gone, at least while you are here," he said.

"Alright," she replied, as they got up and went outside. The church building was a large single building, on property that had a road circling around it. The land and road were about the size of a high school track and field, so from an airplane view, it would look like the church is sitting in the middle of a large park, with a road encircled around it. In the park there are flower gardens, ponds with fish, fountains, and occasional oaks for shade.

As they walked, Humility experienced a suitcase-free walk for the first time in several days. Her friends had briefly carried it for her, but even then, the suitcase still had a psychological effect on her, but now it was gone. As they reached one of the ponds, she saw her reflection in the water and realized she was smiling for the first time since she was shamed.

"This is great, but if I can't leave this place, then the burden is not really gone," said Humility.

"I agree," said Pastor Guidance. "Some people have tried to stay here for weeks, but after a couple of months they grow to dislike this place, and they end up leaving with their burden back in their possession, as well as a hatred for the church."

"So, I'm not the only one to come here with a burden?" she asked.

"Unfortunately, you're one of many," he said. "The Shame Enforcement Officers have many victims, and of course, there are other reasons for being shamed. Many people bring their burdens here, but not as many as I would like. Spirituality by itself does not get rid of burdens, only God can do that."

"I have experienced that," said Humility. "I've been to Spiritual Boulevard and a spiritual block party, but never did I find anyone who could tell me how to get rid of my burden."

"That's because no one can, but God," said Pastor Guidance.

"Then it was God who spoke to me and told me to come here?" questioned Humility.

"Do you still question it?" he replied.

"I am reluctant to accept that there is a God, at least while I am here at this church, because you're going to tell me that religion is the only way to receive his help in getting rid of my burden," she said.

"Why are you so sure that religion is bad for you?" he said.

"Because religion changes you. It turns you into a close-minded person who thinks everyone else is wrong, but many Christians are just as hateful and hypocritical as anyone else. I don't want to be like that," said Humility.

"You don't have to be like that," said Pastor Guidance. "I too don't like many of the ways some Christians express their faith in God, but I don't let that stop me from letting God bless me with his goodwill."

"Are you telling me that the only way to permanently get rid of my burden is to become a Christian?" said Humility.

"I suppose you can say it like that, but that is not the way I would put it," said Pastor Guidance.

"So, do I just sign up, or something?" said Humility. "If I become a member of your church, start following your rituals, paying the membership fees, and calling myself a Christian, then God will take my burden away forever. Is that right?"

"Where did you learn that from?" he asked.

"I picked it up somewhere," she returned.

"The only way for God to take away your burden is in the labyrinth," he said.

"What's that?" asked Humility.

"Let me show you," he said, as they walked further away from the church building, to the back of the garden next to the road, and down stone steps that went into a tunnel underneath it. Up the steps on the other side of the road, they followed a path that led into a large group of tall evergreen trees.

"Are we still on the church property?" asked Humility, noticing that her suitcase was still not with her.

"Yes, this is all a part of our church," he said.

A stone path took them through a thick green forest for several minutes, until they came out into an open field, and then followed the stone path through wild flowers. As they reached the far end, Humility saw a green wall stretched across the field.

"What is that?" she asked.

"Those are Leyland Cypress trees," he said. "They form the walls of the Labyrinth."

"But isn't that a door?" she returned, noticing that a white wooden door was positioned in the middle of the tree hedge wall of the labyrinth.

"Yes," said Pastor Guidance.

"What's on the other side of it?" said Humility.

"I'm sorry, but this is as far as we can go," he replied, as he placed his hand on her shoulder and gently guided her back in the direction they came.

"Why? I thought you were going to help me get rid of my burden," she said.

"I will, if that's what you want, but there are many things I have to explain to you first," he replied. "You cannot just walk into the labyrinth without knowing what's in there and what's expected of you. It is a very dangerous place."

"What kind of danger?" she asked,

"Let's go back to my office, and I will explain it to you, and then you can decide if you still want to go."

When they arrived at the pastor's office, he first explained to her the history behind the creation of the labyrinth. He told her that when the City of Spirituality formed the Shame Enforcement Office, the Church of Atonement was led by God to build the Labyrinth.

"So, it is for people who have been shamed," said Humility.

"Yes," he said. "But I must warn you that once you go inside, there is no way for anyone to go in and save you."

"Really, well, that hardly seems legal," said Humility. "What if someone fell down and broke an ankle or hit their head?"

"Trust me; a broken ankle is the least of your concern in the labyrinth. But to answer your question directly, no one will come in to help you," said Pastor Guidance.

"Why not?" said Humility.

"Well, there is no phone reception in the Labyrinth, and only one person can enter it at a time. I will have no way to be in contact with you, and neither will anyone else. In fact, no one except me will know you even went inside the Labyrinth," he said.

"I could die in there and no one would know," she said.

"That's right, but there is even more danger inside the Labyrinth," said Pastor Guidance.

"How many people have gone into the Labyrinth, you know, since it was built?" asked Humility.

"Many, hundreds," he said.

"And where are they all now?" she asked.

"Some are members of this church. Others are members of other churches throughout the city. However, some choose to leave the Labyrinth prematurely and never get rid of their burden of shame. They did not meet God in there, and he therefor could not take it away."

"Did anyone die in there?" asked Humility.

"Yes, they all died," he said. "For some that was a spiritual death, and then a spiritual rebirth. For others, it was a human death; meaning that they did not let God help them, and the heavy burden of the shame they carried killed the humanity within their soul. The person he or she is today is not even human anymore, but only body cursed to still carry a heavy burden of shame."

"That's terrible," said Humility.

"Yes, it is," said Pastor Guidance.

"But did anyone physically die?" she asked.

"Yes, a few." He said.

"What happened to the bodies? How did you get them out of there? Because you said no one can go in if someone else is still in there. So, how did you get the bodies out?" said Humility.

"The bodies never come out," he said. "And God always informs me as to what happened."

"But what if someone doesn't die?" she asked.

"Everyone dies, as I have already told you," he said.

"Right, I forgot. Some die spiritually and are reborn; some die physically, and others lose their humanity," said Humility.

"Right," said Pastor Guidance. "Which one do you want to experience?"

"Neither," said Humility, with hesitation, and concern for whether the pastor was mentally stable.

"And that means you're not ready to go into the labyrinth," he returned, and then got up from his chair, walked across the room and opened the door.

"What are you doing?" asked Humility, with frustration.

"The city bus will be here soon, and I don't want you to miss it. It was nice to meet you, and I wish you luck. I will show you out," he said.

"But you said the suitcase will show up again if I leave the church property," said Humility, still in her chair.

"Yes, well, that's your problem, not mine," he said.

"But you told me you would help me get rid of my shameful burden," said Humility, as she stood from her chair.

"How can I do that if you're not willing to go into the labyrinth? And how can I let you go into the labyrinth if you're not willing to die?" said Pastor Guidance. "If I let you go in there without you understanding and agreeing with the certainty of your death, then I am as good as a murderer, and I will not do that."

"So, I have to die to get rid of that suitcase?" she shouted.

"Yes," he shouted back. "Now please, leave this church, and a good day to you."

"But I am willing to die," she shouted.

"No, you're not," he shouted back. "The moment I first saw you, I knew you would not be willing to die. I suspected you were too consumed with yourself, and I was right."

"You don't know me," declared Humility.

"You only want to go into the labyrinth to get rid of your shameful burden, isn't that right?" he said.

"Well, yeah, what other reason is there?" she said.

"Listen, I tell you what I will do. Go home, and come back tomorrow, and if you have at least three better reasons for going into the labyrinth, then I will reconsider. Will that work for you?" said Pastor Guidance.

"Yes, I suppose it will have to. Thank you," said Humility, as she walked out of the office, and then out of the church.

"Very well, goodbye," he said.

Humility sat down on the bus bench and waited for it to show up. She realized she was still free from her burdensome suitcase of shame and wondered if it was gone for good. Wouldn't that be great, then she would never have to go into that dreadful labyrinth. The pastor wants her to come up with three other reasons to go into it, but that's impossible.

The bus arrived, and as she was getting on, she tripped and fell on her face. As she hit the steps of the bus, she slid down onto the rocky gravel outside. She got up and tried to get on again, but the same thing happened. Several people on the bus were watching, and even a few were laughing. She glanced around and saw the suitcase sitting there, waiting for her, begging to be carried.

"You've got to be kidding me," she screamed, as she hurried off the bus, and dragged that burdensome suitcase of shame right back into the front door of the church. Then, just as she saw the pastor, the burden disappeared.

"I said, come back tomorrow," Pastor Guidance told her.

"I want to go in, tonight," demanded Humility.

"Why?" she asked.

"To get rid of my burden," she said.

"What other reasons do you have?" he said.

"Truth," she said.

"Truth?" he asked. "What about it?"

"I want to know what true spirituality is. This city has much to say about spirituality, but I haven't heard anything I can believe. I think Christianity, and whatever is in that Labyrinth, will tell me the truth."

"Very well, then, what other reasons do you have?" he asked.

"I, think, that maybe..." she said, hesitating.

"Spit it out, young lady, I haven't got all day," he said.

"The voice of God," she said.

"What about it?" he returned.

"I heard it, I know I did, and it was the best voice I ever heard. I want to hear it again," she replied.

"Good," he said. "Give me another reason."

"Because I want to die," she said, shocked that she did.

"Why?" he asked.

"Because this can't be who I really am," she said. "I think there is more, and I believe I must be spiritually reborn to become that person, and I must die first, shouldn't I?"

"Indeed," he replied. "Very well, then, come on, I will guide you."

Chapter Five

Into the Labyrinth

Humility and Pastor Guidance stood in front of the labyrinth entrance door. It was like any door you would find into a house. The labyrinth hedge wall was about 20 feet high, and the white wooden door and its frame went about a third way up the wall. Standing there, Humility saw the labyrinth as a massive green intimidating presence, and the door was like her, an out of place and small friendly object. She hesitated to open the door, but Pastor Guidance put his hand on her shoulder and encouraged her to be brave.

She opened the door and looked around before she went in. She saw what was like a wide hallway, about the size of the corridor in a shopping mall. However, instead of a floor between the green hedge walls, there was a very swift moving river. She looked to her left (down river) and saw nothing besides the white and transparent river, and the green walls of the labyrinth. To the right (up river), she saw the same thing. But directly across from the door entrance (where she was still standing), she saw the beginning of a narrower, hallway like path, into the labyrinth.

"How do I get across the river?" she turned and asked Pastor Guidance.

"I'm sorry, but I don't know," he replied, and then she looked around for some hidden thing that could help her.

"The river is too fast to swim across," she said, as he came closer to look for himself.

"I agree that it's far, but if you get a running start, then jump as far as you can, then maybe you will be able to swim the rest of the way." He said.

"I didn't know I was going to have to get wet." She said.

"I'm sure that will be the least of your concern," he laughed.

"Should I start from back here?" she asked.

"Yes," he returned. "I will hold the door for you and close it as soon as you go through."

"Thanks," she said, as she faced the door, bent her legs, and prepared to run at full speed toward it. "See you later."

"Good bye, Humility, and good luck," said Pastor Guidance, as humility took off running toward the door. She ran full speed past the door and leaped into the air, gliding over the fast-moving river, toward the other side.

When she hit the water, she plunged in as if she weighed a thousand pounds. The river was warm and comfortable, but the current was so strong that she could do nothing against it. She was beneath, and she couldn't rise to the top. She struggled to swim upward, but the only direction she could manage was down river. Immediately, she recognized her trouble. If she didn't get to the surface, she would run out of breath and die.

It wasn't just the current pulling her fast down-stream that made it difficult to get her head above the water, but also how heavy she seemed. She was no stranger to swimming, which meant that she knew how her weight felt in water. Either she had suddenly increased in weight or the river was thinner somehow than the water she was used to swimming in. After all, she knew that it was more difficult to rise to the surface in fresh water rather than salt water. Maybe the river was another kind of water, one that she had never heard of before.

She was beginning to panic when she suddenly had a great idea. If she could push off the river bottom and launch upward toward to the surface, then maybe she could generate enough force to reach it. She tried to figure out how far down she had sunk, and to her surprise, she discovered she had been sinking gradually. She guessed 20 feet down, but then changed her mind to 10 feet down, but then she had fallen another 10 feet down.

Looking upward, she could see faint green hedge walls on the other side of the river surface, but in-between her and that was the swift blurred water with its alternating white and transparent appearance. Turning her gaze downward, Humility saw blackness, no bottom, and a feeling of despair was beginning to take over. Then, wait, there was a bottom. It was getting closer to her. The river was carrying her along at a racing speed, and therefore she must be reaching a shallower part of the river.

Sure enough, her feet hit the bottom of the river, and she was running along it as the current pushed her. Looking upward, she saw the surface getting closer and closer. It was as if she was running up hill toward it. Then she planted her feet with bent knees and launched upward. Out of the water she shot, like a jumping salmon or tuna she must have looked, but all she was thinking about was the fresh air filling her lungs. She hit the water and sank down again. Horrified, she realized the river was getting deeper again, and then back down she went.

However, with new air in her lungs, Humility became clear-headed and more hopeful. She coached herself to think her way through this. She chose to enter the labyrinth for a reason; four reasons, according to what she told the pastor. She hadn't believed they came out of her mouth when she first said them, but after a moment, she realized her lack of belief wasn't because what she told him was untrue, but because she never saw herself as a religious person. Spiritual, yes, but not religious. Pastor said that she would have to die, but Humility doubted that drowning in the river was what he meant.

She knew she had to die a spiritual death, whatever that meant, but not a physical death. She was about to die a physical death, if she didn't figure out how to get above the water. She wondered how the current of the river kept moving fast when it became deeper, because usually rivers slowed down in deeper parts, but this river kept the same speed no matter what depth. In the last minute or so, she had sunk down to where there was little light from above, with no bottom in sight, and hopelessness was creeping in.

However, just as she was about to run out of breath, she saw the bottom getting closer and climbing up higher toward the surface, just as it did before. Her feet hit the ground, and she began running up the underwater hillside, as the current pushed her along. Then, as the river shallowed, she jumped and glided out of the water, like a salmon, and this time she got a good look at her surroundings before she plunged back in.

She saw the tall green hedge walls on both sides of the river, which looked like a wide hallway of some great building, but instead of a roof above, it was a bright blue sky. She also saw a path that appeared to cross underneath the river, but she couldn't tell for sure. After a few minutes of deep water again, she began to lose hope once more of ever breathing again, and then she found footing on another underwater incline that climbed up until she was able to leap out of the water like a salmon and breathe again. Then, just like before, she was able to look around, but this time all she saw was the green hedge walls.

Again, she sunk down into the deep-dark fast-moving river, and again it became shallow a few minutes later, as she leaped out of the water like a salmon and saw only green hedge walls. This time, when she went down again into the deep water, she lost all hope, and decided to give up. She was exhausted. Four times in ten minutes she leaped out of the water and got air, but only one breath, which was barely enough to stay alive. She felt like she was being dragged into outer space by a rocket and allowed to take a breath from an oxygen tank, just enough to survive.

She was ready to die, so what. If this was all the labyrinth was, forget about it. She would rather die than live off only one breath. Down in the deep-dark, she decided to breathe in the water and drown herself. Was this the Pastor's plan all along, to send her to her death? Was he really a serial killer, who led all his victims into this river death trap? He was right, she was going to die, but not spiritually; physically. She opened her mouth and sucked in the dark-warm river water.

Swallowing water when you're struggling to breathe is one of the worst pains a body will ever endure. Humility's throat and lungs were anticipating a breath of air, so when the water came pouring in, some of it went down into her lungs, and then she began trying to cough it up, but because there was no air, water soaked into her lungs, and her chest seized up as if cement was pouring down her throat and hardening as it touched her lungs. Severe pain, and then she drowned and died.

At least that's what she thought was happening, as her body was floating upward, she wondered if she was ascending to Heaven. Then, as her head reached into Heaven, she felt fresh air, and her lungs began to breathe in the cool air. She was surprised to still be alive, and to be floating comfortably with her head above the water, as if it was like any other river. Not dead; not in Heaven, but still alive in the labyrinth.

How could this be possible? She drowned, but instead of dying, she floated to the surface of the river when before all she could do was sink. She concluded that this was probably due to the strange supernatural attributes of the labyrinth. Taking the water into her lungs must have somehow changed her body in a way that allowed it to float instead of sink, as it did before.

She looked around, as her head and shoulders floated easily above the warm and swift moving river. She saw the familiar green hedge walls, but then she saw a path through the hedge wall on her right, and then she turned around and was shocked to see a door opened with Pastor Guidance standing next to it, with the green field behind him. How could this be? She had gone into a full circle. The river went around in a loop.

"Pastor," she shouted, and waved her hands. "Pastor Guidance." He said nothing and did nothing in return. She didn't really know why she was trying to get his attention, except that maybe he might rescue her. But then she reconsidered. She had to keep going. The hard part was surely over. She drifted right by him, and he still didn't move a muscle. He was as stiff as a statue. She thought it odd, but maybe he did that because he didn't want to disturb her.

Now that she could breathe freely, she could think better about what was going on, without the anxiety of her approaching death. She tried to think about the labyrinth not merely as an obstacle to overcome, but as a way of meeting God and getting rid of her burden. This wasn't just a test or challenge to overcome, but everything had a reason and purpose. Maybe she was never met to die in the river. She didn't know she needed to breathe in the water in-order to rise to the surface and float properly. Who could have possibly known that? It goes against all of a person's survival instincts.

Humility looked ahead, down the river, and saw it turn a corner, as she floated along. Then, as the river turned again, she noticed that another river branched off to the right, but it had a steel gate blocking her from going down it. Water passed through the gate, which was built like the bars of a jail cell, but nothing larger than a small fish could fit through it. She drifted by it, and soon came to the spot she remembered, where a path in the labyrinth went underneath the river, in some kind of tunnel, probably, but she couldn't see it.

There was no way to get out of the river. There was no bank, just green hedge walls. Besides, the river was moving fast enough to make it nearly impossible to grab on to something. She went around two more corners, and then was back to where she first began. Looking up toward the door, she saw the Pastor, still standing there, in the same place he was, like a statue.

"Pastor Guidance, what are you doing still standing there?" she said, but he didn't move a muscle. She kept moving down the river, and around and around the loop; 3, 4, 5, 6, 7, 8, 9, 10 times. Each time, she saw the same thing. Nothing ever changed, and Pastor was always in the same spot, as if he was only a manikin, not a real living person. She had no idea what to do. What was the purpose of all this? Why is she just going in circles, never advancing, as if she was not really going anywhere at all. The moving river made it seem she was going somewhere, but in fact, she was nonetheless stuck in the same place.

This time around, she grabbed onto the gate to climb over it, but as soon as she put her hands on it, a violent shock went through her body, and she was thrown backward into the river. She woke up as she was passing Pastor Guidance again, just realizing that she had been knocked unconscious for nearly an entire loop. The gate had some kind of electrical current that prevented anyone from climbing it.

"This is pointless," she began shouting. "Are you trying to kill me? What am I supposed to do? I can't even get anywhere. How am I supposed to go further into the labyrinth, if I can't even get out of the stupid river? Please help me, I don't know what to do. Where are you? I thought you were going to meet me in here. What kind of game are you playing? Give a sign or something."

Then, as if she gotten an answer, she saw a bright light below her, down underneath the surface of the river. She ducked her head under the water and could see clearly that the light was a floating ball. She swam down, for the water was deep in this part of the river. Grabbing a hold of it, as it fit between both of her hands, she peered into it, and saw words appear. The ball was a mild bluish white light, and the letters of the words were black, as if the light had disappeared in the shape of B-R-E-A-T-H, for that was the first word.

Humility, instantly went up above the water to get some air, but as she went back down to the ball of light, she had already drifted past it, for it must have been fixed in place, somehow, but the current was too strong for her to swim back to it. She drifted around the loop again and was anxious to see the light still in the water. She took a deep breath and went down, but this time she noticed that when she put her hands around the ball of light, the current of the river seemed to come to a complete stop. She wasn't being pulled away from it, as would be the case if it was fixed, and she was not.

She didn't notice this effect the first time she held it, because she had assumed it was free floating, like her. But sure enough, as she held it and read the words appearing inside the ball, she felt no pull on her from the current of the river, as if it had completely stopped. However, the words she read were even more shocking, for they said, "You can breathe underwater."

"How?" she said, in her clearest underwater voice.

"Open your mouth and breathe," said the Ball of Light.

"But I can't; I will drown," she said.

"Did you drown last time?" said the Ball of Light.

"I most definitely did," she said.

"And you're okay?" said the Ball of Light.

"I almost died," she said.

"You did die," said the Ball of Light.

"No, I didn't," she said.

"How do you know?" said the Ball of Light, then suddenly a view of Humility floating face down in the water appeared within the ball.

"That's me," she said. "How long was I like that?"

"Many loops around," said the Ball of Light, as it showed a time-lapse appearance of her floating face down, as she went around and around the loop of the river.

"How?" she said.

"You were breathing underwater," said the Ball of Light.

"I thought you said I died," said Humility.

"Spiritual Death," said the Ball of Light. "Not yet spiritually reborn."

"Really?" she asked.

"Yes; then I changed your physical lungs," said the Ball of Light.

"When?" she said.

"When you swallowed the water," said the Ball of Light.

"I have to go up," she said.

"You don't have to," said the Ball of Light.

"Yes, I do," she said, as she let go of the ball and floated up to the surface while drifting again down river. It was almost too much. The things the Ball of Light was telling her was hard to believe; hard to trust. She didn't want to go through the pain of drowning again. She couldn't do it. She drifted around the loop once more and saw the ball of light floating about ten feet below the surface, in the deep part of the river, and Pastor Guidance was still in the same spot. She dived down and grabbed ahold of the ball of light.

"You're back," it said.

"Where else am I supposed to go?" she returned.

"The gate," said the ball of light.

"What gate?" she said. "Do you mean the gate that nearly shocked me to death?"

"Not with the key," said the Ball of Light.

"What key? Where is it?" said Humility.

"At the bottom," said the Ball of Light.

"Of the river?" she replied. "How far down is it?"

"A long way," said the Ball of Light.

"I can't go down there. It's too far. I can't hold my breath that long," she said.

"I will take you there," said the Ball of Light. "You can breathe in the water."

"I can't," she said.

"You can," said the Ball of Light.

"How?" she said.

"I can help you," said the Ball of Light.

"I have to get more air," said Humility, as she tried to let go of the ball, but couldn't. Suddenly, the Ball of Light took off downward, with Humility dragging along. They raced at high speed to the bottom of the river. Humility was screaming the entire way down, with water occasionally getting into her mouth. When they reached the bottom.

"You're breathing," said the Ball of Light.

"I am," she said. "You were right, but I don't care for your method much."

"I knew what you wanted," said the Ball of Light. "But I had to help you a bit."

"Now what?" she asked.

"There is the key," said the Ball of light, as it shined onto a large key laying at the river bottom.

"What do I do with it?" said Humility, as she held the key in her hand.

"Unlock the gate," said the Ball of Light, then it suddenly disappeared, and the current of the river began to flow fast again. Humility launched herself off the bottom and floated upward and down-river with the current. Her head popped out of the water, and she could see the gate in the distance. The current was moving so fast that when it came time to look for the key hole on the gate, she had time enough only for a quick glance, and then she was taken down river. When the current brought her around again, she dived underneath the water and looked for the key hole. She saw it, but there was no time to put the key in, because the current was too strong. The next time around, she dived down, and quickly fit the key into the hole. As the current pulled her passed it, she lost her grip on the key and was again taken down river. This time around, she saw the gate wide open, and went in.

Chapter Six

The God Fish

When Humility floated through the river gate, she felt free, because something new was in front of her. She had been trapped in a never-ending loop of despair, and more than anything she wanted to get out of the water. Looking around, she saw only green hedge walls. But after a few minutes, she saw the hedge path open into a clearing. It was a large pond. She looked around and saw grass on all sides of the pond, with green hedge walls around and behind the grass. There was nothing else, except a wooden deck that stretched out into the pond. It looked like something a person might use for fishing. She then noticed that a path went from the deck, across the grass, and into a hedge wall path.

Humility was beginning to wonder what she was supposed to do, when suddenly, she realized that the pond had a current going around it. She was being taken around the outside of the pond, in a circle, and she noticed that her position in the water was a little closer to the center. It appeared that the pond had a hole, and the water was draining out of it, which created the current that was taking her around and around. She panicked and began swimming against the current with all her strength. She tried, as hard as she could, swimming both above the water and below it, but the current was too strong.

"What's going on? What am I supposed to do?" she screamed. She wasn't sure if it was the Ball of Light she was screaming at, or

God, or herself, but she got a response, because she saw a light shining down in the whirling pond. She went down and grabbed the ball with both hands. As she gripped it, the current completely stopped, and words appeared within the ball.

"You're doing great!"

"Who are you?" said Humility.

"God," said the Ball of Light. "I thought you'd never ask."

"Really?" she returned.

"Who are you?" said the Ball of Light.

"Humility," she said. "But you know me, because you've been speaking to me."

"I have, but that doesn't mean I know you," said the Ball of Light.

"But you're God; you know everything," said Humility.

"I know about you, but we haven't been properly introduced," said the Ball of Light.

"And how do we do that?" asked Humility.

"Consume me," said the Ball of Light.

"What?" she said. "What does that mean?"

"Eat me," said the Ball of light, as it began to shake and vibrate so much that Humility could no longer hold it in her hands. Then as it ripped from her grip, the Ball of Light dimmed, stretched, and changed shape into a huge salmon. It took off and swam away from her, as the current of the whirl-pool came back and pulled Humility down into a hole at the bottom.

She was shocked at what she just witnessed. Who was this person? This God; this light; this fish; who was he? Is he crazy? Can God be crazy? Is that even possible? Can the creator of everything be a lunatic; a madman? Is he out of his mind? Soon these thoughts were overshadowed by the approaching bottom of the pond. She saw a hole not much larger than her, and she wondered if she would fit. But that's absurd; she can't go down that hole. Where does it go? Where would it take her?

Down the hole she went, down a dark tube-like passage, and after a few frightening seconds she gently spilled out onto the stone floor of an underground cavern. It was a huge wide-open area, about the size of several city blocks. The water from the tube poured out and evenly distributed throughout the cave floor.

For this reason, the water was only a few inches deep, and Humility could stand up and walk easily. It would have been completely dark, if it had not been for a small beam of light on the other side of the cave. As it was, Humility could not see her feet or what she was walking on. She stepped away from the gushing tube, bent down and felt the running water spread out over stone ground, and concluded that she was in a large cave.

She went toward the light and came to its source at about a thousand paces. She found that the light was shining down from a stairwell from up above (outside she presumed). Up the steps and outside she went, seeing the stone slab path of the labyrinth (several paths to be accurate). The stairwell opened to a small circle, with the separate paths heading further in. Standing still, for a moment, she didn't know which path to take. She decided to take another risk of humiliating herself and spoke out loud in a raised voice.

"Which way do I go?" Immediately, she got a response, or at least that was the way she interpreted it. She heard no words, but the path in the middle had a sudden gust of wind blowing out toward her, but not the other paths.

"The middle path it is," she said, while heading down the path. After about a minute in the green hedge hallway, she came out into a wide clearing with a whirlpool and wooden deck. In fact, she realized it was the scene she had seen a few minutes earlier. Humility followed the path across the grass and stepped out onto the deck. Leaning against its railing was a long fishing pole with a shiny chrome spinning lure.

She considered this for a moment and wondered if this fishing pole was meant for her. Who else could it be for? She hadn't seen anyone else so far, and the Ball of Light did tell her that she had to eat it, then it transformed into a fish. Maybe she was supposed to catch it and eat it. Humility thought this was an absurd line of thinking.

Besides, she didn't know how to fish, and she certainly didn't like the taste of it. She stood there for a while, looking utterly confused, and too embarrassed to ask God what to do. That was who she had been speaking to when she had shouted, but this time she didn't want to do it.

"You look confused," said the voice of an older man.

"You scared me," said Humility, startled by the sudden voice of a strange man in a strange place. "I didn't know anyone else was here."

"Where?" he said.

"Here, in the Labyrinth," she returned.

"Is that what you call it?" he replied. "I don't call it that."

"What do you call it?" she asked.

"A pond," he said.

"Well, I didn't mean just that, but also the hedge paths as well; the Labyrinth," she said.

"I see," he said. "For you it's a labyrinth, but I know my way around, so I never call it that, because I always know where I am going."

"You're teasing me," said Humility.

"A little," he said, laughing. "I know what this place is, of course, but I do not know who you are."

"My name is Humility, and who are you?" she said.

"Evangelist is my name," he said.

"What's that?" she asked.

"It means someone who shows people how to know God," said Evangelist.

"That's why I am here," she said. "I spoke to God earlier, or at least I think I did, and he told me that to be introduced to him I must consume him."

"It is true. You spoke to him. No need to doubt it," said Evangelist. "He is a fish in this pond, and you must catch him, kill him, and eat him."

"It seems very strange," said Humility.

"It does, because it is strange," he said. "But, it is the only way to be truly introduced to God, in the Labyrinth, that is."

"I thought you said you didn't call it a labyrinth," she said.

"Well, there you go," he laughed. "I eat my words."

"Better than eating fish," she replied.

"Not this fish, I assure you," he said.

"If you say so, but how did you get in here?" she said.

"I live here," he replied.

"Oh," she said. "Do you know anything about fishing?"

"I do," he replied. "Would you like me to show you?"

"Yes, please," she said.

"Alright, let me see," he said. "Let's talk about the pond for a moment. What do you know about it?"

"I know the water comes in from the river, then goes down a hole at the bottom of the pond, and then dumps out into an underground cave," she said.

"That's right," said Evangelist. "The water then gathers into an underground river and springs upward until it eventually feeds back into the river. The God fish is swimming against the current right now, look, you can see him if you look closely. Can you see him?"

"Yes, I see him," said Humility.

"Now, this pole is what you will use to catch him," said Evangelist. "You will hold the pole like this, with two hands on the grip, your thumb on the line in the reel, and the pole held high over your head. You will reach back and then launch the pole forward, casting the lure into the pond, as you gently release the line from the reel."

It took Humility several minutes to practice casting the lure out into the pond before she could do it correctly, and then she was fishing. Evangelist showed her how to reel the lure in slowly, and how to set the hook when the God Fish bites. She was casting and reeling in for quite a while before she realized that Evangelist was gone. She was all alone, casting, reeling, and fishing for the God Fish.

After about a hundred casts, she was beginning to feel as if she would never catch him. She saw him swimming near her lure, but he never took a bite. She felt stupid, because she was no fisherman, and probably looked stupid doing it. She also didn't like that it was called a fisherman. Why can't she call herself a fisherwoman? She knew that no one called a woman that, but she thought it was unfair.

She was beginning to get bored. Wasn't she supposed to be seeking to know God and get rid of her burden? Fishing? Really? Why? Couldn't she meet God some other way? This labyrinth was strange and not at all what she thought it would be. Then suddenly, her fishing pole nearly bent in half, and she struggled to keep it in her hands. The pressure was instantly taxing on her strength and endurance. Between the strength of the salmon and the current of the pond, the stress upon Humility's back was almost unbearable, and the pole was about to snap.

The line from the reel was zipping out from the spool and Humility had no idea what to do. She couldn't reel in at all, and at the rate the fish was taking line, it would run out soon, and the fish would be gone. Then, suddenly, with a great pull, the fish jerked the pole right out of Humility's hands, and it went flying into the pond. She was stunned. How could this be? This wasn't supposed to happen. Who cares about fishing, that's not what bothered her, but rather the fact that now she couldn't introduce herself to God. It was over. She failed.

"Evangelist!" she shouted. "Evangelist, where are you? Evangelist, help me."

"Yes, what is it," he said, as he came running out of a path in the hedge walls. "Did you catch him?"

"No," she panicked. "I lost my pole."

"Well, you can't catch the God Fish without a pole," he replied.

"Is there anything that can be done?" said Humility.

"There's always something to be done," said Evangelist. "There's always hope."

"You don't think the pole is still attached to the fish, do you?" asked Humility.

"I'm certain it is," he responded. "That's no ordinary fishing line. Not the everyday sort you would find in a tackle shop. What you've got there is stronger than steel. It's called Grace Wire, because its strength was not crafted by the art of human hands, but by God himself."

"Do you mean that God made the fishing line?" said Humility. "Why?"

"I think he made it for those who aim to catch the God Fish. I suppose he wanted to make sure that we had strong enough fishing line to catch the strongest fish in the world," said Evangelist.

"Then, maybe, if I jumped into the pond, I could grab ahold of the pole again," she suggested.

"Yes, I think you're right, but you won't be able to swim back to shore, because the current is too swift," he said.

"Then I should take the pole with me," said Humility.

"Yes," said Evangelist. "Reel the God fish in from down below. That's ingenious. The current and downward force of the pond will work in your favor, and when he comes flailing out of the tube, make sure you kill him right there and then, before he turns into something else."

"What do you mean, turn into something else?" she said.

"Well, the God Fish has been known to transfigure into other creatures when he senses he's about to die," said Evangelist.

"Like what?" she asked.

"Like a fire breathing dragon, or a raging bull with the power to bring down mountain walls," he said.

"How do I kill him?" she asked.

"Here, use this," said Evangelist, as he pulled a small club out of his back pack.

"You want me to beat it over the head, that's barbaric," said Humility.

"If you know a better way to kill him, then by all means," he said.

"How will I hold the pole with both hands and also hold the club?" she said.

"Tuck it into your belt," he said.

"Right, that will work. Well, here I go," she said, as she tucked the club into her belt and climbed over the railing and jumped in.

Under the water it was clear but spinning. She saw something coming toward her, what was it? It was too big to be a fish. It looked like a rock or a piece of steel. As it got closer she did see something animal-like. A huge mouth with sharp teeth. Suddenly, she realized this was a bad idea. The terrible creature was coming straight at her, and probably going to bite her. She turned and tried swimming away, and thankful that she could still breathe under water.

She was making good speed, and when she looked back, she saw that the fish was not gaining on her as fast, but still gaining. Looking across the pond, she could see the fishing pole being dragged far behind the salmon. Her only chance was to get the pole in her hands, before the fish caught up to her and took a bite out of her. She had to swim across the center of the pond, but the current would most likely pull her down into the cave. It was worth the risk, because the awful creature was almost at her toes.

Quickly, she cut across the middle, just as the salmon snapped at her feet and missed. As she reached the center, the tornado like current was so strong. She struggled, vigorously, frantically, and then failed. Down she went, into the hole, and through the tube, until she spilled out onto the dark cavern floor. Determined this time, she marched across the cave, up the stairs, down the middle path, and out into the grass. Looking around, she wondered if anyone was watching, because she felt oddly that someone was, but she saw no one. Up over the deck railing she climbed, but before she jumped, she looked first to see where the fish was at. After a moment, her eyes adjusted, and she saw him easily. He raced by her, along the outer edge of the pond, and then Humility jumped in.

There it was, coming like a bullet toward her, the fishing pole. Reaching out her hand, to get ready, she felt the grace wire (the fishing line that connected the pole to the fish), and it cut deep into her palm. She let out a horrific scream, but there was no time to be in pain. With her other hand she reached out and caught the handle of the fishing pole as it was going by. She re-gripped the pole, with one hand above the reel, and the bottom of the pole handle placed against her hip. With her other hand (bleeding), she swam painfully toward the center of the current, hoping to get sucked down the hole at the bottom as soon as possible. She got her wish, and when she spilt out onto the cave ground again, she repositioned the pole and began pulling in the God Fish.

Facing the hole in the cave wall, where the pond water poured out, Humility reeled him in, but the fish was still tugging back with all its strength. Humility was winning the fight. Then, the God Fish spilt out with the water, right at her feet, and she didn't know what to do. Remembering the words of Evangelist, if she didn't kill the fish quickly, he would turn into some other kind of horrible beast.

Grabbing the club in her belt, she hesitated. There wasn't much light, and she didn't know where the fish was at. Reaching down, and bending at the knees and waist, Humility felt for the fish, and was shocked to find him nearly as large as her. Light suddenly illuminated from him, but it wasn't friendly light. Small flames of fire rushed out of his mouth. She knew he was probably transforming into a dragon, so she held the fish with one hand on its back (the best she could, for he was very large), and then blasted the God Fish in the head with the wooden club.

Screams; sharp piercing cries, sounded from the fish, and Humility hesitated. But when flames and light grew as the fish grew, she knew she had to keep hitting him, or he would turn into a dragon and burn her alive. With both hands on the club, from high above her head, she came down hard on its head; 2, 3, 4, 5 times. But then she stopped as her stomach went into knots and hair stood on the back of her neck. She no longer heard wild animal cries, but those of an infant. She heard sounds of a baby dying. What was this? This cruel torment; why? She couldn't kill a baby. But then she remembered that he wasn't a baby; he was just a fish. And she had to kill him and eat him, so she could be truly introduced to God.

Holding the wooden club up high, she prepared the killing blow, but the sounds were eerie, because they were that of a human child; a baby. Humility reached down to feel for the fish, but what she felt startled her. She dropped the club and ran toward the stairwell. When she got there, and began climbing the steps, she ran into Evangelist (literally), who held an oil lantern in his hands. Humility fell to the ground, sobbing. Evangelist was startled, but he had seen this response before. It was never the same, but everyone always struggled to grasp the sheer nightmare of killing the God Fish.

"There, there, Humility, I am here to help you get through this," he said.

"I will not go back there," she sobbed.

"It is not as bad as you might think," he replied.

"It's horrible," she yelled. "He's not a fish; he's a baby. I hit a baby. I won't kill him."

"He's already dying," he returned. "The question is: do you want to be introduced to God?"

"This is sick!" shouted Humility. "Why didn't you tell me this was going to happen?"

"You wouldn't have understood," he said. "If I told you everything about the God Fish, without you experiencing it, you would misunderstand and run away. Many have done that very thing, and never met God, truly."

"I'm not killing a baby," she said. "I am certainly not eating a baby."

"I assure you, he is only a fish. He transforms, yes, but his nature is a fish. That's why he is called the God Fish. He is a fish, but he shows you much more than that. He shows you what God did for you, and me, and all people," said Evangelist.

"But I felt him. I heard him," said Humility.

"Come, I will show you," he told her, as they walked over to the fish, and he shined his lantern light on the scene. Humility saw lots of blood, and a twitching, almost dead salmon.

"You promise that he's only a fish," pleaded Humility.

"Yes, I promise," he said. "Now, finish him. Kill the God Fish."

"Why? You said it's already dying?" she asked.

"It might not be dead for hours, if you don't finish it now. Do you want to wait that long?" he said.

"I suppose not," she returned. Then she lifted the wooden club and delivered the death blow. Suddenly, the light went out, and Evangelist was gone. She called for him but got no response. She felt horrible. Why was this supposed to be good? Killing a creepy fish; how was that going to introduce her to God?

Chapter Seven

The Way to Perfection

Humility was kneeling in the ankle-deep water of the underground cavern, with one hand on the bloody wooden club, and the other on the very large dead salmon. It looked as if she was mourning a dead friend she had just lost. She wondered why this beautiful creature had to die. She knew why, essentially, which was so that she could be introduced to God, but she wondered why killing this fish was the requirement to do so. Then, as if someone had turned on the lights, the cave became suddenly bright, because a huge bonfire was burning at the center of it. It was too hot. Humility could feel intense heat, and she jumped up to her feet, wondering what was going on. On the other side of the fire, she saw a tall white-haired woman, standing too close to the flame.

"Bring it over here," said a proud, but soft, yet easily heard voice. It was coming from the woman by the fire.

"Excuse me," said Humility, as she went closer to talk to the mysterious woman.

"Could you bring your fish over here?" said the woman.

"He's not my fish," said Humility, who was not certain if she should call him her fish.

"He's not?" asked the woman.

"Well, I killed him, but that doesn't make him mine, does it?" said Humility, but all she got in return was laughter; bright, joyful, and even silly laughter.

"You have nothing to be ashamed of, daughter," said the woman. "You should feel honored. You have just done the highest thing a human could ever do. You have slain the God Fish. Congratulations! But we have to cook him, don't we, if we are going to eat him?"

"You're going to eat him with me?" asked Humility.

"Of course, I am, and others as well," said the woman.

"But who are you?" said Humility.

"My name is Grandma," she said.

"Not my Grandma," said Humility.

"I am everyone's Grandma," she replied.

"Okay," said Humility, confused as what to say next.

"What is your name?" said Grandma.

"Humility," she returned.

"Don't just stand there, granddaughter, bring me your fish," said Grandmother.

Humility went to where the fish was at, and saw it for the first time, up-close, and in the light. It was silver like a wedding ring, with dark-blue patterns throughout, like little pebbles sparkling in the river. There was also hints of red sunset, as if twilight was upon the fish. Humility felt deep sorrow, because twilight had indeed come upon the fish, and then night, forever. Now that the deed had been done, she wished she had not done it. She wasn't proud; not honored, as Grandma had suggested, but ashamed. If she had the choice to do it again, she would have declined. She wanted to meet God, but at what cost? What kind of God would require the death of such a beautiful creature?

She also wondered if the God Fish meant that it was God of all fishes. The greatest fish the world had ever known, living secretly in this labyrinth, and now it was dead. She had killed the King of King Salmon. How could she do it? She remembered seeing the fish swimming toward her in the pond. Sure, at that moment, he looked like he was going to kill her and eat her. But that doesn't change how she felt, now, after knowing how great he really is. Maybe he had the right to kill and eat her. Maybe that's what should have taken place.

Didn't this creature have more of a right to eat her, than she had the right to eat him? He was a lordly fish, but she is not. She is just a person; just Humility.

After thinking all of this, she felt a hand on her shoulder. It was Grandma; she had come to her side. "Everything alright?" she said.

"I don't want to do it," said Humility.

"I know, it's tough to see him in this state," said Grandma. "So amazing; so kingly; so magnificent. But don't worry, it isn't the end, you know."

"For him it is," said Humility.

"No, the God Fish is alive," said Grandma.

"No, he is dead," said Humility.

"For you, he is dead, but for me and everyone who has eaten him, he is alive," said Grandma.

"Are you being serious?" asked Humility, looking a little irritated.

"Yes, but you have to trust me, some things are more than what they seem," said Grandmother.

"If he is dead to me and not to you, then his life is not bound to this body. It has a soul," said Humility.

"One could say that not only does he have a soul, but he is the source of all souls," said Grandma. "He is dead, compared to the way he was living a few moments ago, but life is still in his flesh. And you could be certain, that the God Fish will be swimming that pool every time another person comes looking to meet God."

"Then, he is not dead?" said Humility.

"He is dead," said Grandma. "But he is not dead forever. By killing him, you nor he has lost anything, but gained. You will learn from your experience, here, that there is more to life and death than you currently understand."

"That makes it a little better, to know that," said Humility.

"A little?" asked Grandma.

"A lot," said Humility.

"Good. Do you think you can carry it over to the fire, now?" said Grandma.

"Yes," said Humility.

"Great, I will meet you over there. I'm going to get some things from my kitchen to prepare the God Fish for cooking," said Grandma.

Humility struggled to get a grip on the giant salmon. Then, she figured out what all fishermen know, that grabbing a fish behind his gills, at the jaw, is the best way to carry him. She dragged its heavy body close to the fire, but it took longer than she thought it would. She had to take a few brakes along the way. The fire had cooled down and gotten smaller; just right for cooking. Grandma was standing there, waiting for her, with a knife on a large white table.

"Put him up here, Humility," said Grandma.

"I can't pick him up that high," she responded.

"You can. Give it a try," said Grandma. "I will help you."

Together, they lifted the huge salmon onto the table, and Humility watched as Grandma cut all the meat from the bones, skin, guts, and head. She then placed the meat into a large rectangular steel black box, closed it, and threw it into the fire's bed of coals. There, the fish baked. The rest of the fish she threw into the flames to burn. Humility sat and waited in silence, because Grandma left to go to her kitchen. Later, Grandma came and took the box out of the fire with long wooden dowels and removed from it the cooked salmon. Carrying it on a large plate, Grandma took it to the kitchen, and Humility sat waiting and thinking about what all this meant.

What did it have to do with being introduced to God? Is this what Christianity really is, killing and eating a fish? What does this have to do with getting rid of a burdensome suitcase of shame? How much more of this labyrinth must she go through? She had many questions, and desperately wanted answers. She hoped that Grandma could give her some answers when they eat the God Fish. With perfect timing, Grandma showed up at her side and invited Humility into her house.

"You live here?" asked Humility.

"Oh, yes. I have a little apartment right here in the Cavern of Salvation," said Grandma.

"So, that's what this place is called," said Humility, as she followed Grandma to a wall in the cave, where a wooden door opened into a hallway, then into a large sitting room, with five people sitting around in comfortable chairs and sofas, talking and laughing. Grandma told everyone that dinner is ready, and led them into a dining room, with the meal already laid out on the table, and the God Fish was its center piece.

"Let me introduce everyone," said Grandma, as everyone took a seat at the table. "This is our guest of honor, Humility, who killed the God Fish." At this introduction, everyone stood and began clapping and giving congratulations, and Humility also stood, but not knowing what else to do or say. Then Grandma continued with the introduction. "Humility, you already know myself and Evangelist. The other four are Ms. Faith, Ms. Hope, Mrs. Love, and Grandpa. He is my husband, and the six of us are your welcome-party here at the beginning of your conversion to Christianity."

"My conversion?" asked Humility. "Is that what this is?"

"My child, don't be afraid of the word conversion, or the idea of it. If you prefer, you can call it being introduced to God, officially," said Grandpa. "They are the same thing, because once a person truly meets God, he or she is immediately converted, in the heart that is. To meet God, is to receive everything you've ever truly desired. Though, it doesn't come all at once. Like a starving person, who when he finally gets to eat and drink again, does so in small doses, not quickly, to avoid cramps."

"I see," said Humility. "Conversion is the spiritual food a person receives after spiritually starving?"

"Very true," said Grandma. "And that's why we eat the God Fish at a person's conversion, because it carries with it a symbol of what is literally happening, though unobserved by eyes and ears."

"That's right," said Grandpa. "In the labyrinth, the God Fish is a symbol, but a symbol put into literal physical form. So that, in other words, if you kill and eat the God Fish, you will meet God, but if you don't, you will not meet God in the way that really counts."

"Why is that?" asked Humility.

"Faith can answer that best," said Grandma.

"Well," said Faith. "It's because the only way to meet God is to be perfect, and no human is perfect; that I don't think anyone would disagree with. God is perfect, and if anyone tried to enter his presence without being perfect, he would never be successful, because God would never allow it."

"Why not? I mean, I let people become my friends who seem to be worse than me," said Humility. "Am I friendlier or more loving than God?"

"I can answer this," said Love.

"Please," said Faith.

"I'm sure you are a very loving person, as we all are," said Love. "However, God's love is perfect, and our love is not. Would you agree that your love is not perfect?"

"I agree," Humility said, with a humble smile.

"Then, since God's love is perfect, he cannot let anyone contaminate it," said Love. "If God let someone come into his presence and exchange love with him, without the person having perfect love, then that exchange would be tainted, like the mixing of clear water with dirty water. Even if the water was only a little dirty, it would still taint the water it mixed with, and therefore that water would no longer be perfectly clean. God cannot let this happen, because he is perfect in every way. A perfect person is also a perfect guard against his own destruction. That is, he perfectly guards against anything that would take away his perfection in any way. Therefore, it's only because your love is imperfect that you can befriend other imperfect people."

"I've never thought about it like that," said Humility. "It makes me sad, because it seems that God is so perfect that he can't love us."

"Well said, Love," said Grandpa. "Hope, I believe you might have something to say."

"Thanks, there's hope for us," said Hope, and at this everyone smiled and laughed, even Humility. "There's hope in Jesus Christ."

"Wait a minute," said Humility. "I'm sorry for interrupting."

"No, it's okay," said Hope. "Go ahead."

"Well, I have heard this kind of statement before," said Humility. "People say there's hope in this religion or that; this wise person or that; this philosophy or that. But how can any person solve the problem? How can anyone make us perfect? I'm sure people try to become perfect, but no one has ever been successful, at least as far as I have observed."

"Very good; you're right," said Hope. "We live on earth, amidst other imperfect people, which means it would be impossible to become perfect while we are here. In other words, how can dirty water become clean while being within a tank of dirty water? How can something become clean while dwelling in a dirt pile or garbage dump? That might seem harsh to compare people to dirt and garbage, but compared to perfection, I don't think it's a bad example."

"You're right," said Humility.

"There's even more problems with a person trying to become perfect," said Love.

"Share it with us," said Grandma.

"Even if a person was able to leave this sinful world, without anyone or anything else to influence it, that person would still find it impossible to become clean, because he or she is still dirty; still imperfect; still a sinner. How can an imperfect mind become perfect while being imperfect? In other words, how can imperfect water become clean without any help from outside of itself?"

"Very good," said Grandpa. "If a person is by himself, he will not have anyone perfect to help him become perfect. And since there are no perfect people on earth, then it will do no good trying to become perfect here or somewhere else, not the moon or mars or anywhere that exists."

"Maybe there are perfect aliens out there; you know, extra-terrestrials," suggested Humility.

"There most certainly is," said Faith. "God is the greatest of them all. Now we come to the point. Jesus said, 'My Kingdom is not of this world.' In fact, his origin goes even further than that. Jesus is God. The creator of space, time, and matter became a human being."

"Really? Why?" asked Humility.

"To make us perfect," said Faith. "To save us from our sins. Another way to put it is that he did it to save us from our imperfections (which is what sin means), by making us perfect."

"Are you saying that Jesus is the Creator of the Universe, and he became human to save humans from our imperfections, by making us perfect?" asked Humility.

"That's right," said Faith.

"And by eating the God Fish I will receive such salvation? I will become perfect?" asked Humility.

"Yes," said all six of the others at once, and laughter and joy followed.

"Well, what are we waiting for?" said Humility, with a great big smile on her face. At this, they passed around the corn, mash-potatoes, green-beans, gravy, rolls, butter, fruit-salad, green-salad, and the main dish, the God Fish (which was Chinook Salmon). During this time, some of them asked Humility about what she had done so far in the labyrinth.

Then Grandma prayed, "Dear, Heavenly Father, Lord of everything, God, we thank you for this meal. Satisfy us with your presence and nourishment. Fulfill us, as we eat for our physical bodies and our spiritual bodies. And answer our questions," prayed Grandma.

"LORD, give us faith, and give Humility faith. Bring to power the faith she already has. Bring her to life. In the river she gave in and died to herself, with Christ, and now she wants to be born again when she eats the God Fish," prayed Faith.

"Show her your perfect love, in Christ, who loves her in such a way that he would be crucified on a cross, and shamed, for her sake," prayed Love.

"And he fulfilled her hope and ours by coming back to life. Bring Humility spiritually back to life, and in time, her physical body will come back to life after it dies. Be her hope through all difficulty and suffering, my Lord, Jesus Christ," prayed Hope.

"And Jesus, our Savior, we eat and fellowship in your name, amen," prayed Grandpa, and the others, including Humility said amen as well.

"You can now take the first bite of the God Fish," said Grandma.

Humility took her fork and put a piece of the fish in her mouth. She ate with joy and expectation, but as it went down she felt nothing, except that she wanted more. Looking at everyone, they observed her for a moment, and then began eating too. Humility ate all the God Fish on her plate and touched nothing else. She was a little embarrassed to put more God Fish on her plate, but the others encouraged her to do so. They explained that most of the fish was for her to eat. The first time is always intense. A new Christian, in the Labyrinth, cannot get enough God Fish, until his or her stomach is so full that it is about to burst at the seams, like a bag stuffed too full.

"I do feel amazing," said Humility, when she slowed down her eating. "May I ask when I get to meet God?"

"You can meet him now," said Evangelist, who had not spoken to Humility during the conversation.

"I will show you to the Spiritual Greeting Room," said Grandma.

"Okay," said Humility, who had suddenly become so nervous that she began to tremble. Grandma hugged her and guided her to a special room, to meet God. They stopped outside the door.

"Are you ready?" asked Grandma.

"No, I'm not," said Humility. "What is this room? Am I actually going to meet God; like physically, face to face, in person? Am I going to meet Jesus?"

"Yes, that is all correct," said Grandma. "I don't know how to answer your question about what the room is, because it is a very special room, and I can only explain it by using somewhat technical words. The room has capabilities that are not found anywhere but here in the labyrinth. It's sort of a combination of scientific technology and theological power. No, that's not the right way to explain it. It's rather, where science and miracles come together. No, that's not right. God made all scientific technological advancements possible, because he created everything. Listen to me ramble on. Are you familiar with the concept of dimensions?"

"Like the warping of space-time due to gravity, in the fourth dimension of space?" said Humility.

"Right, like that," said Grandma. "This room is a severe warping of space-time. From other things that I am not sure I understand well enough to explain to you."

"That's okay," said Humility. "I think I get it."

"You do? Great," said Grandma. "Any other questions?"

"I don't think I am ready." said Humility.

"No one ever really is," said Grandma. "It still shakes my knees whenever I go in there."

"Do you go in there often?" asked Humility.

"No, not often, because there are so many wonderful ways to have fellowship with God, that are not quite so intense. Besides, after you've experienced the presence of God in such an intense way, all other experiences are quite fulfilling," said Grandma.

"Is he really the Creator of the Universe?" asked Humility.

"Yes, he is," said Grandma. "I know, it's just as scary as it is exciting."

"He's perfect? What is perfection like?" asked Humility.

"You'll have to see for yourself, don't take my word for it," said Grandma. "But if you need some encouragement, I will tell you that perfection is foreign. It's like what meeting a total alien from another planet would be like. But it's also familiar, because he's human. I mean, God's not human, but he became human. Could you imagine meeting God in some kind of other form? That would be rough. He's like a baby, but even more innocent. He's also like an old wise person. He's beautiful."

"Alright," said Humility.

"You ready, then?" asked Grandma.

"Yes," said Humility, then Grandma opened the door, and Humility walked in. The door shut behind her.

Chapter Eight

Dancer

Humility walked into the darkness of the spiritual greeting room, but soon she realized it was not a dark room in which she was walking. The sun was rising slowly over the horizon. It was only morning wherever she was at, not evening, as it was in the labyrinth. One thing was sure, as she looked around, she was no longer in Grandma's apartment within the cave. Humility seemed to be in a new and strange world. She saw almost nothing, and the light she could see from the sky, seemed other worldly. It wasn't the normal orange, pink, blue, and white. All light seemed blue to her, and the sky was moving and twisting in ways that it never did on Earth. What was she standing on, because it seemed as if she was floating upward toward the sky? Light from the rising sun was getting brighter and brighter.

She could see the surface of the sky. It wasn't like the sky at home, with an atmosphere, but something else. Humility was floating up to it, and about to touch it. It became thin and clear; she could see something on the other side of it. Then, she broke through, like bursting out of the water, into the open air. But wait, that's what she had done. This was water. She was in the ocean and had just swam up to its surface. She couldn't see her body. Where were her hands and feet? Suddenly, she realized she had been transformed into a fish. Oh, how fate turns. She was the fisher before, but now she was the fish, and someone was about to catch her.

This must be the truth. Humility was almost certain that she had it right. She had become a fish and now God was going to catch her. She knew this had to be right. Of course it was. Payback time. Revenge, and it was God who was going to have the last laugh. She thought that she had done something great; something honorable by catching the God Fish, but at what cost? Now she was going to meet God, but not the way she thought. God was going to catch her and eat her. Humility could even feel the hook and line that was pulling her. At first, she had figured she had freely swam upward, but now she knew; she had been reeled in by The God Fisher.

All her worries were confirmed when she saw the boat. Reaching out of it were the two hands of The God Fisher, grabbing her and pulling her into the boat. But wait a minute, what was really going on? She realized that when she first came through the surface of the ocean, out into the open air, her eyes had been blinded by the brightness of the morning sun. It was the true sunrise, not the much dimmer blue light she saw from down in the ocean. Now, her eyes were beginning to adjust, and her confusion was disappearing. Sitting in a small row boat, she saw a young handsome man in the front and she was on the other end, in the back.

"I'm not a fish," she said, suddenly. At first, she thought this was a most liberating statement, as if she had just realized she was still alive, and anyone who would have heard it would have joined in on the celebration of the statement. However, when she saw the face of the man looking at her, as if he was looking at a silly little girl, she suddenly felt differently.

"No, you're definitely not a fish," he said.

"I have legs, and arms," she said, as she looked at herself with her newly adjusting eyes.

"Yes, I just pulled you out of the water," he said. "I saved your life, because as you were swimming, several sharks were approaching, and they didn't look friendly."

"But I felt the hook and line pulling me," she said. "I was a fish, and you were the fisherman."

"Was I?" he laughed and smiled, radiating all the world with his joy, at least Humility thought so. She couldn't help but smile and laugh herself.

"Who are you?" she said.

"I am he," said the man, and by now Humility could see fully that he was young, strong, dark skinned, with black hair, and green eyes. Humility remembered she had come here to meet God.

"You're God?" she asked, with curiosity and wonder. But it wasn't really him that made her curious, but rather the bright green water and white coral reflecting from below the surface. They had drifted into the shallows, and she looked and saw jungle-land with palm trees. Everything was so bright and beautiful, because they were at the tropics. She wondered why God appeared to be a native of a remote pacific island. He was shirtless, his shorts seemed to be made of leaves, though masterfully woven, and his boat was a carved-out tree. Humility was also wearing a bathing suit, and it was made in the same way that his was.

"I am, but please just call me Dancer, that's what everyone calls me around here," he said.

"Dancer?" she laughed, and so did he. "Why Dancer?"

"It's my nickname, since I was a little boy," he said. "From the moment I opened my eyes, I moved and shook to the rhythm of the music. Here, music is everything. It is the foundation to every aspect of our culture. When I began to crawl, I did it with a dance. And when I could walk I learned all the traditional dances, but then I created my own. I was willing to dance all my own choreographs, no matter what other people thought. Some were good, and some were very silly, but I didn't care, because I loved to dance. It was then, when I was about nine years old, that people started calling me Dancer. We're all dancers here, but I got the nickname, because I did it more than anyone else."

"Do you still dance?" asked Humility.

"Of course, but not as much as in my youth. Now, I try to live my whole life as one Great-Dance," he said.

"How do you do that?" she asked, as the boat bumped gently against a grassy bank, shaded with palm trees.

"Just like a dance, every step I take in life, every move I make is intentional and planned. Though sometimes, like dancing, I occasionally make up something new on the spot, but always in good form. Dancing is beautiful and skillful, and so should life be the same. Dancing brings me joy, and it also brings joy to everyone who sees me do it, and so it goes with my life," he said.

"That's so cool," said Humility. "I didn't realize life could be so much fun."

"Of course, it most definitely can, even in the City of Spirituality," said Dancer.

"People can be shamed in my city, even for dancing, if it goes against the laws of social status. I was shamed twice, for suggesting my own spiritual opinion over a more authoritative man," she said.

"Yes, I know," said Dancer, and he looked sad. "I know why you did it, too."

"I'm not even sure I know why I did it," said Humility.

"It was for me that you did it," said Dancer. "Though, I don't think you knew it was me specifically. You did it for truth, and authenticity, and integrity, and justice, and love. All those things, when you put them together, you get me, don't you?"

"I guess so," she said.

"It was me who guided you to the Bible and spoke to you," said Dancer. "Well, it was me in Spirit. It was I who guided the beggar lady to speak to you."

"Really? Why?" asked Humility.

"I wanted to awaken something within you that has fallen asleep," said Dancer.

"And what is that?" she said.

"I will tell you, later, I promise, but even more important than that, I want to dance with you," said Dancer.

"No way," she responded.

"Why not?" he said, smiling. "You said you wanted to be introduced to me, well this is me. My name is Dancer, remember?"

"Yes, I do want to, but I don't know how to dance," she said, smiling right back to him.

"That's okay, I can teach you," he said. "Watch, it's easy; this is how you do it."

He put one foot on each side of the boat, in the bow, where it was narrow, and he began rocking the weight of his body back and forth to the rhythm of a song he was singing. It was a light hearted and cheerful tune, but the words were in a language Humility could not understand. He started moving his arms from side to side (slowly, with the rocking of the boat). He was bending his knees down low and then rising as the boat rocked back and forth. Then he began moving toward her, as he kept dancing. He reached down and pulled her up to her feet. They were both smiling and laughing, as he guided her, and showed her how to dance.

"What does it mean; the words you are singing?" she asked him.

"It is a story about a man and a woman, on a little boat, like this one, who fall in love during a dance," he said, with a beaming smile.

"Wow," was what came out, but in fact, she didn't know what to say. No one had ever made her feel like this before. "Why are you singing it?"

"Because I like it," he said, and she became embarrassed, having asked it. How could she think it had anything to do with her? It was just a song that happened to come into his mind.

"I like it too," she said, hoping she hadn't offended him for asking.

"Good, because I wrote it about you," he said.

"Me?" she said, and her eyes grew huge. They were still dancing. "When did you do that?"

"When you were born, mainly, as a celebration of your birth, but I also wrote some of it before that, and some right now, on the spot," said Dancer, as he lifted her up off her feet, and jumped to switch positions with her, both landing where the other was previously standing, on the edge of the boat.

Humility never danced much, but whenever she had, it was simple movements. Now, she was dancing with this master dancer (who happened to be God), and they were balancing on the edge of the small row-boat, rocking back and forth, and it was fun. By herself or with anyone else, she knew for sure that she would have tripped and fell into the water, but not with him. Dancer was a good name for him, because he was excellent, and his smile was seeping into her, like the way sunshine seeps into your skin, and the joy was overwhelming. She wanted to call him, The Great Dancer, but then she did trip on her clumsy feet, and went tumbling overboard. However, her hands never left his, which meant that she had pulled him out of the boat with her. Anticipating their plunge into the water, they hit, but never went in.

"We're dancing on top of the water," she said excitedly.

"Yeah, isn't it amazing?" said Dancer. "I won't let you go, if you don't let me go. We can keep dancing. Nothing will stop us, I will make sure of it if you want to."

"Yes," she said, and that's all she could say because she was speechless. Unexplainable joy was rushing through every inch of her body, even deep into her soul. They now glided across the water, even as it slightly swelled and fell as oceans do. The style of the dance had changed. Dancer was now spinning her, dipping her, gliding with her, hand in hand, as if they were dancing center stage at a grand ballroom. She looked quickly at her clothes and saw that she was no longer in a bathing suit, but wearing a beautiful red dress, like rose petals in both color and texture. She was wearing glass slippers, like Cinderella, and as her eyes lifted, she no longer saw the sun, the ocean, or the island, but a grand white ballroom, crowded with familiar faces.

"Who are these people?" she asked, as they continued dancing.

"Everyone you've ever loved or respected, and even those from whom you've wanted love and respect, but never received," said Dancer. She saw her parents, and her best friend Modesty, and her grandparents, but also the Shame Enforcement Officers who had shamed her, and the Ridiculer and his girlfriend. Also, members of the council of the City of Spirituality. She saw Pastor Guidance, and many others.

"Are they really here? I mean, is that really them?" she asked, but deep down she thought she already knew the answer, because her grandparents were dead, and her mom and dad would never come to a ballroom dance.

"It is only an experience, but a real experience as far as you and I are concerned," said Dancer. "I am real, and you are real; therefore, this is all real for us, but the people you see here are not experiencing this, as we are, so it is not real for them."

"I like it," she said, as she clung to him in a dance that was more like an embrace, with her arms around him and her head on his chest. He was wearing what looked like a dress-uniform of a soldier. It was white, with medals hanging above the right breast pocket.

"Good," he said, as he knelt to one knee in front of everyone, bringing from his pocket a little box. He opened it and revealed a diamond ring. "Because I want to ask you something. Humility, will you marry me?"

"Marry you?" she said, shocked. "But how? How does someone marry God?"

"Marriage to me is not like a marriage to a human," said Dancer. "We won't have a house, or a bed, or children together, but we will have a life together. I will be your husband, and you will be my wife in all other ways. I will never leave you, and I will take care of you always. I will be your best-friend, your protector, and your soul-mate. I will be yours and you will be mine. You will be the apple of my eye; the greatest desire of my heart, and I will be your knight in shining armor. We will build a life together, and no one will do greater things than us, nor be happier than we will. I will never hurt you. I have prepared a home for you with no tears or sin. It is perfect, in Heaven."

"Really?" she asked, shocked and surprised.

"Yes, because I love you," said Dancer. "Do you love me?"

"I think I do," she returned.

"Is that a yes? Will you marry me?" he asked again.

"Yes," she said, and then he put the ring on her finger, in front of everyone.

"Why are they all here, if they are not real?" asked Humility, but even though they were not really there, it felt good to see them. She didn't quite know what the feeling was. She tried to pin point it. Was it courage, confidence, honor, or satisfaction? It must be all of the above.

"They are here for you," said Dancer. "The way you feel when seeing them, it is real, and you can have it completely, much more than you do now, in the City of Spirituality."

"Really?" said Humility.

"Yes, my soon to be bride," said Dancer.

"When will we be married?" asked Humility.

"Soon, but first we must demonstrate our devotion to one another," said Dancer.

"I will do anything for you," she said, and she hardly believed she had said it, but it was true. She loved him, and would be his bride, even if she had to fight a dragon or seek a treasure on the other side of the galaxy.

"And I will do anything for you, my love," he said. "Nothing will stop me from becoming your husband, if that's what you truly want."

"It is, with all of my heart," she said.

"Then we cannot fail," said Dancer. "But it won't be easy."

"Anything," she said. "What must I do?"

"Finish the labyrinth," he said.

"If you are with me, then I can do it," she said.

"I know you can. And when you reach the end, we will have our wedding," he said. "I will be with you, but not always as you see me now."

"What do you mean?" she asked.

"I will be invisible," said Dancer.

"Invisible?" repeated Humility. "Do you mean that I will not see you, but I can touch you and hear you?"

"You won't be able to observe me at all with your five senses," he said. At these words, a single tear began to fall down Humility's cheek. Dancer wrapped his arms around her and took her away from the ballroom, where they could be alone. It was a small room with brooms, mops, dusters, and other cleaning supplies. A small reddish light was illuminating the room, shining from a large rosy-like stone that hung around Dancer's neck, on a silver chain. He took it off and put it around her neck. "This will give you physical light when you need it, and the ring around your finger will be a physical reminder of my devotion to you. But my spiritual presence, which is now inside you, is far greater than any material object."

"How will you be present inside me?" asked Humility, still crying.

"When you ate the God-Fish, I entered your soul, forever," said Dancer.

"But I would rather have you with me, like you are now, so that I can see you, and hear you, and feel you," cried Humility.

"Yes, and so would I," said Dancer. "But my Spirit is enough for us both. He is me and I am him. You will get used to him. He is with you now, and he always will be. If he is with you than I am also with you, though not as a man, but as an invisible person. It is in your thoughts where you can make contact with him. Even though he is in your mind, don't believe for a second that he is any less real. You will be able to recognize the difference between his thoughts and yours, because you know me, and I am not you. If you hear thoughts that are more like me than you, then it is me. Got it?"

"Yes, I think so. I will try," she said.

"Good, I love you," said Dancer.

"I love you, too," she returned.

"Give this to Grandma," he said, as he handed her a note.

"Okay," said Humility, as they hugged. Then he opened the door and she went through it.

Chapter Nine

The Power of God

Humility saw Grandma standing on the other side of the door. The door closed, but Humility couldn't except it. She didn't want to depart from Dancer. She couldn't breathe without him; not for a second. She loved him. But how could this be? She wondered why she felt so strongly about a person she just met. Turning around, she gripped the door handle and reopened it. Eagerly anticipating seeing Dancer standing there, her smile was immediately ripped from her face, as she stepped back into the spiritual greeting room, which had been transformed into an open sky.

Humility was falling now, and far below her was the land of some unknown country, but above her she saw the door she fell out of, as it was flying away. Bewildered, she realized that the door was on a moving jet airplane. Then, she saw Grandma leap out of the airplane, with a thick cord attached to her waist. Catching up with Humility, Grandma wrapped her arms and legs around her, and someone else began pulling them to the jet. When they got back inside and closed the door, Humility saw that they were not in a jet, but in a dark room, and it was Grandpa who pulled them back in. The airplane was a reality within the spiritual greeting room, but not on this side of the door.

"Grandma, what was that?" said Humility.

"I was about to ask you the same thing," she returned.

"It's broken," said Grandpa.

"I know," said Grandma.

"What's broken?" asked Humility.

"The Spiritual Greeting Room is broken," said Grandpa. "When we pulled you out, it broke, because whenever two or more people are connected by something physical, between two different time dimensions, the doorway between the dimensions will always break. We were connected by the cord I used to pull you both in, and therefore time had been disturbed, and the spiritual greeting room is now broken."

"That sounds serious," said Humility.

"It is," said Grandma. "Why did you go back in, Humility?"

"I wanted to see him again," she returned.

"Is that what God wanted?" asked Grandma.

"No," said Humility. "But I wanted to see him once more."

"You didn't want to leave him, and that's why you went back in, isn't it?" said Grandpa.

"Yes, I'm sorry," said Humility.

"You're not the first one to feel that way," said Grandma. "You must learn to do what he tells you, even if your love for him overpowers your obedience."

"I understand," said Humility. "I acted foolish."

"Don't worry, he will build us another spiritual greeting room, if that is what he wants," said Grandpa. "Nothing we can do will ever destroy what God wants to do; it will just send it down another path."

"What do you mean, another path?" said Humility.

"The labyrinth is not what it was a few minutes ago," said Grandma.

"What does that mean?" said Humility.

"Time has changed," said Grandpa. "Let me explain. When you entered into the labyrinth, was Pastor Guidance with you?"

"Yes," said Humility.

"After you entered the labyrinth, did you see him? Was there anything unusual about him?" asked Grandpa.

"Yes," said Humility. "No matter how much time went by for me, Pastor Guidance never moved a muscle, as if he was a statue."

"That's because this labyrinth is in a different dimension of time than the City of Spirituality, and the reality of time perception in which you have always known. In fact, based on your description of the pastor, I bet your entire time in the labyrinth will go by, and not even a single moment will go by for him. When you go back, no time will have gone by for everyone else, but for you it will have been days, or weeks, or however long you stay here," said Grandpa.

"Seriously?" asked Humility.

"And when you went into the spiritual greeting room, to meet God, you were also in a different time dimension," said Grandpa. "How long were you in there, the first time?"

"I don't know," said Humility. "Maybe an hour or two."

"For us, it was two years," said Grandpa.

"Two years," panicked Humility. "You're joking."

"No, I'm not," said Grandpa. "But that was what God wanted, because he planned it that way. When you went back in, against what he told you, you opened the door into a completely unplanned and unknown time dimension in the spiritual greeting room. On top of that, when we connected the cord between the two times, to get you back, we broke the door and disturbed the relationship of time between there and here."

"Are you saying that more time could have gone by, without us knowing about it?" said Humility.

"Yes," said Grandma. "Look around, our house is dark, but there is still a small light coming from somewhere out there."

"Where does it come from? Not from our lamps," said Grandpa.

The three of them walked toward the light, all the while, bumping into chairs and tables, not seeing them in the dim light. They could feel and smell dust, as if no one had lived there for a very long time. The light was coming from the open front door, that went out into the cavern. Out in the middle of the cave was a small fire pit. Grandpa knelt down to feel the ground, but it was dry, no water. It was silent. Only the burning fire could be heard, no rushing water was gushing in from the pond above.

"It's dry," Grandpa whispered. "No water."

"Where is it?" said Humility.

"I don't know," he returned. "Dried up, maybe, or dammed and redirected somewhere else. It's been a while since we were here last, but I don't know how long."

"But where can the water be?" asked Humility.

"Why don't we ask her," said Grandma, pointing to someone walking toward the fire, with a bundle of wood in her arms.

"Hey there, mam, where is the water that once poured into this cave?" asked Grandpa.

"Water," said the woman, as she threw what was in her arms into the fire. "In this cave; never was any water."

"Yes, there was," said Grandma. "We should know; we used to live here."

"Lived here, impossible," said the stranger. "I was born here, and I've always been here. My folks died, but before I was born they lived here. My Ma was born here just as I was, and so was her Ma. It's a tradition for us Hopi's. Name's 33 Hopi, but just call me Hopi; please to meet you. And who might you three be?"

"I'm Grandpa; this is Grandma, and her name is Humility," he said. "Your name is familiar to me."

"It is?" said Hopi.

"Yes," said Grandpa.

"You know this woman?" said Grandma.

"Well, no, but I think I know where she gets her name," said Grandpa.

"Where?" said Humility.

"Do you remember the four people who ate dinner with us; Evangelist, Faith, Hope, and Love?" said Grandpa.

"I think this woman is a descendant of Hope," said Grandpa. "It makes sense, if you think about it. Hope would never have given up on the idea that we would return. She must have waited for the rest of her life in this cave and raised her children here. She must have passed down the tradition of waiting for us, to her children. She passed her name down to her daughter, and her daughter did the same to her daughter. The name Hope must have slightly transformed into the name; Hopi."

"That's quite a theory," said Grandma. "But we don't know if it's true. If it were, it could mean that 50 years has gone by."

"50 years," said Humility. "That can't be right."

"We should be so lucky," said Grandpa.

"What do you mean?" said Humility.

"It could be much more," said Grandpa.

"Hopi, is any of what Grandpa said, true?" asked Grandma.

"I don't know, it's rather strange," said Hopi. "Ma told me a story when I was a child, and it sounded something like that, but I never believed it. I don't wait for anyone to come back, but my Ma may have. I didn't wed or have children either, so I guess the tradition dies with me."

"Or maybe it's fulfilled with you," said Grandpa.

"I don't think so," said Hopi.

"Tell me, Hopi, why is your name 33 Hopi? What significance does 33 have?" said Grandpa.

"I'm the 33rd generation of Hopi's," she said.

"Oh my," said Grandpa, as he did some math calculation with his fingers.

"What?" said Grandma.

"Do you think that we've been gone for 33 generations?" said Humility.

"Yes," said Grandpa. "Could be as long as a thousand years."

"That's impossible," said Humility. "There's no way. I refuse to believe it."

"I think she has the right idea," said Hopi. "You people are crazy. I don't know where you came from, but I would appreciate it if you left my cave. The door and stairwell are over there. Please go."

"Fine, if you want us to go, we will," said Grandma, as the three of them walked away. They were each thinking that Hopi was very unkind to tell them to leave. They needed help. What would they do? They were confused and without much hope. It had abandon them.

"She was a most unhelpful person," said Grandma.

"I guess the tradition is dead," said Grandpa.

"You don't actually believe that theory of yours, do you?" said Grandma.

"I think he may be on to something," said Humility, as she reached the top of the stairwell first, and looked around at how different everything was from what it was the last time she stood in the same place. She remembered there being a hedge wall labyrinth higher than her head, and three separate paths were visible from the stairwell, but not this time. She saw only a wasteland.

"What happened?" cried Grandma, with tears running down her cheeks. "It's all gone. Our beautiful labyrinth is dead."

"There, there, my dear wife, don't be sad, we can get it back," said Grandpa.

"How?" cried Grandma.

"Maybe God will bring it back to life," said Humility.

"Do you really think so?" asked Grandma.

"Sure, he can do anything. Why not?" said Grandpa.

"I bet he will make us a new one," said Humility.

"Maybe she's right," Grandma said to Grandpa.

"I think she is," said Grandpa.

"I almost forgot, Grandma, Dancer told me to give you this," said Humility, as she took out of her pocket the note Dancer gave her and handed it to Grandma.

"Who is Dancer?" both Grandma and Grandpa asked at the same moment.

"That was his name, in the spiritual greeting room, God," said Humility.

"Oh, that's a wonderful name for him," said Grandma. "Let me read the note. It says, 'Dear, Grandma, don't be discouraged about the labyrinth. Trust Humility, her instincts are right. Do whatever she tells you to do, and make sure she continues onward in the labyrinth. As for you and Grandpa, I want you to take up your residence again in the cave and continue your work. Train Hopi as your apprentice, and I will send her a husband when she is ready. Remember, I am with you; God.'"

"Wow," said Grandpa. "He knew this was going to happen."

"Of course he knew," said Grandma. "He's God, isn't he?"

"Yes, he is. And he knows everything," said Grandpa. "I'm just surprised, that's all."

"What do we do now?" asked Humility.

"You heard what the note said, didn't you?" said Grandma. "We should be asking you the same question."

"I don't know what to do," said Humility.

"Sure you do," said Grandma. "You said God could restore the labyrinth, and I think he wants to, because he said that we should make sure you continue in it."

"So, we should ask him, then, I think," said Humility. "Is that what you Christians call prayer?"

"What we Christians call prayer," repeated Grandpa. "Listen to her. You're a Christian too, Humility."

"I am?" asked Humility.

"Most certainly," said Grandma. "So, go on and pray. Talk to God, or Dancer, whatever you want to call him."

"Okay, just give me a moment," said Humility, as she turned around and put her hands over her face. She wanted to block out everything the best she could, just her and him. Then she spoke quietly into her hands. "Dancer, are you there?" She didn't hear anything, but she thought something. The word yes was in her mind, but she wasn't quite sure whether it was just her thoughts or him. "Dancer, is it really you? How can I be sure?"

"It's me. Have courage," she thought, and decided to trust that it was him communicating to her.

"Hi," she spoke into her hands.

"Hello Humility. You don't have to speak out-loud if you don't want to. Just think what you have to say, and I will receive it just the same," said Dancer.

"Okay," she said, in her thoughts. "Do you want me to continue on in the labyrinth?"

"Yes," he responded.

"Okay, I thought so, but it's not here anymore," she said. "Can you bring it back?"

"Yes. Do you want me to do it right now?" asked Dancer.

"Please. Thank you, Dancer," said Humility. "And Dancer."

"Yes," he returned.

"I am sorry about going back through the door," she said.

"I forgive you, and I know you did it because you love me," he said. "But now you know that what I say is for your blessing, and what I don't say is not a blessing, but a curse. Don't worry, though, I can break all curses."

"Thank you, Dancer," she said.

"You're welcome, Humility. I have something I want you to do for me," he said.

"Anything," she replied.

"I want you to bring back the labyrinth, using my power, the power of the Spirit of God that flows through you," he said.

"Really?" she said.

"Yes, I want you to turn around and command the labyrinth to rise and come back to life. Hold your arms out and command it to happen, in the name and power of the Spirit of Jesus Christ," said Dancer.

"If you want me to, I will," said Humility.

"Good, sweetheart, talk to you later," he said.

"Okay, goodbye," said Humility.

"Did you pray?" asked Grandma.

"Yes," said Humility.

"Great, so did we, but we're not sure if God's going to do it," said Grandpa.

"He will," she responded.

"Really? When?" asked Grandma.

"Right now," said Humility, as she reached out her hands and began speaking. "Desert, you have no power to stay what you are. You have no power over God. You cannot hold back the labyrinth from rising from the dead. So, labyrinth, I command you to rise and live again, in the name of the Spirit of Jesus Christ. Come back from the death that took you and be a miracle; be a living labyrinth once more."

When she said those words, the dirt beneath her feet, and as far as her eyes could see, began to shake and tremble. The earth was quaking, and a thunderous sound was roaring. Suddenly, lightning shot out of her hands and struck the ground in many places. Then, green cords flung from her fingers and attached themselves to nearly every inch of the desert. After only a few seconds, Grandma, Grandpa, and Humility realized that this strange miracle was the labyrinth being rebuilt. The green cords were forming green hedge walls, and the quaking ground and flashing lightning that preceded it had been the necessary energy and reformation of the soil. A minute or so later, the labyrinth had been completely rebuilt, though not exactly the same as before.

"What was that?" said Grandpa, though it was obvious that he knew what it was, but he didn't know what else to say.

"That was God, working his power through Humility," said Grandma.

"He told me to do it," responded Humility; explaining herself.

"He gave you an incredible power," said Grandpa.

"Yes, but she should never do it unless he tells her to," said Grandma.

"I don't think I could if I wanted to," said Humility. "It was just for the labyrinth. It's not magic. It's God's power; he let me borrow it for a moment."

"He sure did," said Grandpa. "The labyrinth is back. Unbelievable."

"What now?" asked Humility.

"You must continue in the labyrinth," said Grandma. "I don't know what you'll run into, but you can handle it. You're with God now. Remember, you can talk to him anytime you like. Just seek him in your mind. Talk to him, as if you would talk to anyone else. This is called prayer. Did you have a burden before you came into the labyrinth?"

"Yes," said Humility. "A burdensome suitcase of shame."

"Yes, of course you did," said Grandpa. "Don't worry. That is probably the next thing you will do in the labyrinth. God is going to take it away, forever."

"Good, I want to get rid of it," said Humility. "Are you guys coming with me?"

"No, remember what the note said. God wants us to go back to the cave," said Grandma.

"Right," said Humility. "Well, thanks for everything. Will I ever see you again?"

"Of course," said Grandma.

"Goodbye Granddaughter," said Grandpa. "Good luck."

"Thanks, goodbye," she said, as she hugged them both. They went back down the stairwell into the cavern, and she took the path to the right.

However, a little way down the path, she turned around, came back, and then walked down the center path. She wanted to see if the pond and river was as it had been. She took the center path and followed it to the pond. Seeing everything as it was the last time she looked at it, she was satisfied, but wondering if she would see Evangelist, even though she was not sure if God had brought him back as well. She went back to where the stairwell and the three paths met, and then she walked back down the right path.

Chapter Ten

Burden Gone

She followed the path further into the labyrinth, and first came to a large steel gate. It blocked the entire path, and Humility looked to the other side to see if anyone was standing there. She saw a small person standing at military attention, and completely covered in iron armor. Then she observed the little armored soldier begin marching from one side of the path to the other; again, and again, while shouting "1-2, 3-4, 4-1-2, 1-2-3-4."

"Excuse me," said Humility, trying to raise her voice over the little shouting soldier. "Hello; excuse me. Soldier, excuse me."

"What is that?" screamed the Little Soldier, suddenly pulling a sword out and holding it high. "Who's there? Stand back, or I will chop off your head."

"Chop off my head, that's a terrible thing to say to someone," said Humility. "Put that thing away. Why on earth would you act in such a way to someone you've never met?"

"I will ask the questions," said the Little Soldier, and Humility could tell it was a little girl underneath all the armor, by the sound of her voice, and her general attitude.

"Who are you?" asked Humility.

"I told you that I will ask the questions," said Little Soldier Girl. "Who are you, and why are you trying to break into the gate?"

"I'm not trying to break into it, I would much rather you let me in," said Humility.

"And why would I do that?" said Little Soldier Girl. Humility had to think about this for a moment before she could give a response.

"Because I need to keep going," she said.

"Keep going where?" said Little Soldier Girl.

"In the labyrinth," said Humility.

"Yes, but why?" said Little Soldier Girl.

"I suppose, if I were to give a direct answer, God told me to keep going, and I need for him to get rid of my burden," said Humility.

"Well, why didn't you just say that to start with," said Little Soldier Girl, as she opened the gate and took off her helmet. She was a red haired, baby-faced, ten-year-old girl, with a tiresome look in her eyes.

"Why is this gate here?" said Humility.

"I thought that would be obvious," said Little Soldier Girl. "It's here to stop you from going further."

"Yes, I figured that much, but why would anyone want to stop me?" said Humility.

"You would want to stop you if you knew what's down this path," said Little Soldier Girl.

"What?" said Humility. "What's down there?"

"Something awful," said Little Soldier Girl. "The Shame Enforcement Officers."

"You're joking, right?" said Humility.

"No, I am not," said Little Soldier Girl, very seriously.

"The real, Shame Enforcement Officers?" asked Humility.

"Of course," said Little Soldier Girl.

"What are they doing here?" said Humility.

"What do you mean?" said Little Soldier Girl. "They are here for you."

"For me? Why?" panicked Humility. "I don't want them."

"But they are here, and you must face them," said Little Soldier Girl.

"Face them; are you crazy? No way," said Humility. "I want to get rid of my burden, not add to it."

"You don't have to be rude," said Little Soldier Girl, who was beginning to cry, and Humility remembered that she is only a child.

"I'm sorry," said Humility, as she put her arm around Little Soldier Girl. "You're not crazy. I'm the crazy one. What's your name?"

"Courage," she said.

"Well, that's a wonderful name," said Humility. "You are very brave, and I am happy to have met you."

"Really?" returned Courage. "Am I brave? I do try to be brave, and bold, and brawny, and burly, like a big, brutal bear."

"Brilliant usage of the 'B' sound," said Humility. "Your name should be Brave."

"It is," she replied. "Courage is my family name, but when I'm not on duty, people call me Brave."

"Really," said Humility, who was looking like she didn't know if the girl was telling the truth about her name.

"Yes, mam," said Brave. "Now, about the Shame Enforcement Officers."

"I'm sorry, but I don't understand why they would be here," said Humility. "What good can it do?"

"It is what will get rid of your burden," said Brave.

"What? I thought God is going to do it," said Humility. "It can't be the Shame Enforcement Officers who get rid of my burden."

"It's both," said Brave. "It's the only way. This is why we keep the gate closed, because some people aren't ready. But you said you wanted to get rid of your burden, so I let you in. If you're not ready to face the Shame Enforcement Officers, then you should go back."

"Go back where?" shouted Humility.

"I don't know," cried Brave, who began sobbing. "Wherever you came from. It's not my fault. You shouldn't take it out on me."

"Wait, I'm sorry. I didn't mean to say it like that," said Humility.

"So, you're not mad at me," said Brave.

"No, of course not," said Humility.

"Then why won't you just go," said Brave. "Why are you making it so difficult? You're making me cry. It's only my first day guarding the gate. And look how awful I am doing."

"What good will it do?" said Humility.

"Fine, give me a moment," said Brave, as Humility watched her turn around and begin a conversation with someone, but she could not see who it was.

"Alright," said Humility, but all the while she was wondering if Brave was having a nervous breakdown, as some kids mildly do, because she was certainly talking to herself, in a conversation.

"She isn't ready," said Brave.

"Give her another try," said the voice of someone who Humility thought she recognized. It sounded like Dancer.

"Maybe she should start over," said Brave.

"She's just confused," said Dancer. "She'll get the hang of it."

"Dancer?" said Humility, interrupting the conversation.

"Yes," said the voice of Dancer, but it was in her head, so that no one else could hear it. "I've always been here. I've never left. Don't you want to get rid of your burden? Do you still trust me?"

"Yes," said Humility, aloud, so that Brave could hear it.

"What?" said Brave. "Yes what?"

"Yes, I will go," she replied, and in her thoughts, she had a wonderful conversation with Dancer, as she walked down the path toward the Shame Enforcement Officers. The gate, and Brave, were now far behind her, no longer in sight.

"Humility," said Dancer. "They're just around the corner."

"Who?" she said.

"The Shame Enforcement Officers," he returned. "And unlike the ballroom dance, where they were not really there themselves, this time they will be."

"What do you want me to do?" asked Humility.

"You have my permission to use any power of mine, but the problem you're going to have is that you have not learned very much of it," said Dancer.

"What can you teach me, right now?" she asked.

"Remember this, then," said Dancer. "Anger is a strong fuel for the use of any one of my powers, but finishing the power requires other expressions, such as love or forgiveness. People who have tried to finish using anger as a motivation have not had good results when they confronted their own burdens."

"What do you mean by finish?" said Humility. "Finish what?"

"The confrontation, which in your case is the Shame Enforcement Officers. You must confront them about what they did to you, so you can get rid of your burdensome suitcase of shame," said Dancer.

"How can being angry and then loving, help me confront them? That doesn't sound like a miraculous power, to me," said Humility.

"That's because it's not the actual power, but rather a way for you to mentally control it," said Dancer. "The real power is that you will nearly be able to do anything to them."

"Really?" said Humility. "How do I use this power?"

"I am giving it to you right now," said Dancer. "All you have to do is say the thing you want to happen, aloud, and it will happen."

"Wouldn't it be easier to just think it, and not say it out-loud? They're going to hear me and know that I am the one doing it," said Humility.

"That's the point," said Dancer. "It's all a part of getting rid of your burden. You'll see."

"Okay, I'm ready," she said.

"Good luck," he returned.

She went around the corner and immediately saw three men standing there, smoking cigarettes in their shame enforcement uniforms. They seemed to have no idea they were in a labyrinth. By the content of their conversation with each other, Humility listened and confirmed that they believed to have just wandered into a secluded park in the City of Spirituality. And that's exactly what happened, but with a little help from Dancer, the labyrinth and the park were unified by some kind of spiritual worm-hole, or at least that's what Humility called it. They also had no idea that they were being observed by someone.

"Your cigarettes are no longer lit," spoke Humility in a tone that seemed to be advising them of something that went wrong with the cigarettes.

"Oh, I didn't know anyone was there," said one of the Shame Enforcement Officers. "You startled us. You're right, they aren't lit anymore. Thanks."

"You're welcome," said Humility. "You'll have a difficult time relighting them, because your lighters don't work."

"She's right," said a different Shame Enforcement Officer who was trying to light his cigarette with his lighter. There were three of them.

"Sure is," said the third Shame Enforcement Officer, who also couldn't get it to spark a flame.

"How did you know that?" said the first SEO.

"I know a few things," she said.

"What else do you know?" said the third SEO.

"I know that you're standing on one leg," she said, then he immediately put it down, not knowing why he had done it in the first place.

"That's a silly thing to say. Of course you know, you're watching me do it, aren't you?" said the third SEO. "But do you know what's going to happen in the future?"

"Yes," she replied.

"Like what?" said the second SEO.

"In thirty seconds, you're going to slap the other two officers in the face," said Humility.

"That's absurd," he returned.

"Is it?" said Humility, pausing for a moment, and then she spoke again. "You are slapping them both in the face."

All four of them were shocked (including Humility), to see it happen. He slapped them both. Of course, she believed Dancer, when he said that she will have this kind of power, but now she actually saw it happen, and her belief was confirmed to be real. What could she do with such power? What did God want her to do with it? Confront the Shame Enforcement Officers, but how? Certainly, making them slap one another was not all that was to be done. She had to speak to them about what they did to her; but how?

"What did you do that for?" said the first SEO to the second.

"Are you trying to start something?" said the third SEO.

"No, I promise, I'm not," said the second SEO. "I didn't mean to do it. I don't know why I did it. That woman made me do it, somehow, I think."

"You think she used some kind of magic, do you?" said the first SEO.

"Could be," said the second SEO.

"You're not getting off that easy," said the third SEO. "Come here, I'm going to slap you back."

"That was a little harder than I slapped you," said the second SEO, after the third SEO hit him in the face.

"Did you cause that to happen?" the first SEO asked Humility. "Did you just use magic on us?"

"Do you remember me?" she said to all three of them.

"Wait a minute, are you that girl we shamed a few nights ago, and then again at the spiritual block party?" said the third SEO.

"All three of you were there, right, both times?" said Humility.

"It is you," said the third SEO.

"What are you doing here?" said the first SEO.

"Are you following us?" said the second SEO.

"You can't do that," said the first SEO. "We could arrest you. What is the meaning of this? Why are you here? Where is your suitcase?"

"It's gone," said Humility, and when she said it, she realized what had just happened. She didn't even mean to do it, but it happened. Because she had the power of God to do almost anything; therefore, when she declared that it was gone, it came true. The suitcase of shame is gone, and she knew it at once. And just like that, the thing she had to do was done, but she wasn't sure if this was what Dancer had intended.

"Now listen to me, the three of you," said Humility. "You were wrong to shame me. You should have never done it. I did nothing to deserve it."

"Nothing to deserve it, of course you did," said the first SEO. "You broke the law of social status. Who do you think you are talking to us that way?"

"You don't tell us what is right, we tell you," said the Third SEO.

"You extended yourself above the authority of a man in a spiritual conversation, which is illegal," said the second SEO.

"It is illegal only in a corrupt spiritual society," said Humility, but in her thoughts, she asked Dancer if that was a good thing to say. He told her it was perfect, and that he supports her in standing up against the laws of social status in the City of Spirituality.

"Corrupt spiritual society is it?" said the first SEO.

"That kind of talk about our great city is also illegal," said the third SEO. "She will have to be shamed again."

"I agree," said the second SEO. "But this time the shaming will have to be permanent, and very severe."

"Yes, you're right. Let's get her into custody, first, and then we can decide what to do to her," said the first SEO, as the three of them moved toward Humility to put her in restraints.

"You're not going to touch me," said Humility, and suddenly they stopped and couldn't come any closer. Humility decided it was time to see what these powers could do. "All three of you are on your stomach."

"You can't do that to us," said the first SEO, who was now on his stomach.

"How did she do that to us?" said the second SEO.

"She's a witch, with magical powers," said the third SEO.

"I'm not a witch," she responded. "These powers are from God. I am a Christian."

"Let us go or being shamed will be the least of your concerns," said the third SEO.

"I don't think you guys are in a position to make threats," said Humility.

"We have the entire government of the City of Spirituality on our side," said the second SEO. "Do you really think that being put on our bellies changes that. Eventually, you will pay for what you are doing to us, and for your resistance of the laws of social status that govern our great city."

"Get up," said Humility, then each of them did. "I am going to change those laws. I am going to confront the Council of the City of Spirituality, the same way I am confronting you, right now. I am going to change things."

"What makes you think that you, a girl, barely an adult, can stand-up to the council? What power do you have to change anything?" said the first SEO.

"I have the power of God," said Humility. "To prove it to you, watch what I can do."

Suddenly, the first and second SEO observed the third SEO change his entire demeanor toward Humility. It was after she said to him, "You are my friend and greatest protector. You serve me now, not the City of Spirituality." Upon hearing this, he went and stood next her, appearing to now be on her side.

"I am done serving the corrupt laws of social status," said the third SEO.

"What? Are you serious?" said the second SEO.

"Get back over here," said the first SEO.

"No, I now serve her," he replied. "If you have a problem with that, feel free to come over here and stop me."

"You are mind controlling him," said the second SEO, to Humility. "What right do you have to do that?"

"I have the only right, which God gave me," said Humility. "Who are you to say who does or does not do the will of God?"

"Well, that may be your belief," said the first SEO. "However, whatever you do, by mind controlling people, it won't be real."

"Maybe your right," said Humility, as she released the third SEO from his service to her, by saying, "Go back to being a Shame Enforcement Officer."

"Are you with us?" the first SEO said to the third.

"I don't know," he replied. "I suppose I am, but I am very confused.

"Now, let us go," said the second SEO.

"You realize, with this power, I can dismantle the entire system of the City of Spirituality and the laws of social status, with just a few words," said Humility.

"That won't happen, because you know that taking people's true choices away from them is not real-life, but something you made to fit what you think is best," said the first SEO. "But the council doesn't do that, they do only what the people want."

"So, you think people want to be shamed, do you?" said Humility.

"Not those people, of course. Some have to be shamed," said the second SEO. "The rest of us prefer it that way, you know, to keep the piece. To have order in the City of Spirituality."

"You shamed people for speaking the truth," said Humility.

"Is that what you think you did?" said the third SEO.

"It is not truth, to challenge the spiritual authority of a man. It's nothing more than a lie," said the second SEO.

"That's right, you deserve what you got," said the first SEO.

"I've heard enough of this. You three, out of here. Go back to the City of Spirituality," said Humility. When she said those words, suddenly, the three Shame Enforcement Officers vanished.

"Well, that was interesting," said Dancer, in person.

"You're here," said Humility, as she gave him a big hug.

"Yes, I am here," he replied. "And you've finished the labyrinth. Well, we still have to walk out of here, but that won't take long."

"And what about our wedding?" said Humility.

"It's waiting for us, on the way, you'll see. But we have to go back to another path," he said, as the two of them turned around and went back toward the gate.

"I didn't do such a good job with the Shame Enforcement Officers, did I?" asked Humility.

"You did great," said Dancer. "Why do you doubt it?"

"I barely confronted them," she said.

"But you did confront them, and that was all I asked you to do," he replied.

"You said I should have shown love toward them, but instead I sent them away," she said.

"Sometimes, the most loving thing you can do is send people away, if that's what they need," said Dancer. "There will still be time to do more."

"There will?" said Humility.

"Oh yes, on the other side," he said. "In the city."

"Like what?" she asked.

"You're going to be a part of the change."

"What change?" she said.

"The transition; from the City of Spirituality to the Fabled City," he said.

"What's the Fabled City?" she asked.

"It's the Perfect City; the only one of its kind, but that won't happen until much later. But the transition is happening now. You are the spark that will light the fires of spiritual revolution," said Dancer.

"Me?" said Humility.

"Yes. Look, we're at the gate," said Dancer, and then they saw the little soldier girl called, Brave, who was collapsed against the hedge wall, sleeping. "She is so adorable, isn't she?"

"Yes, she is," said Humility, as Dancer opened the gate and the two of them went through. A few minutes later, they reached the stairwell that went down into the cavern, where Grandma and Grandpa live, but they kept walking, taking the third path, the one that Humility had previously left unexplored. They soon arrived at a great wide-open field, and with what looked like thousands of people standing and waiting for them to arrive.

"Who are these people?" she asked him.

"They are heroes of faith," he said. "All of them have already lived their sinful lives, and now live in eternal glory, in Heaven, with me."

"These people have died; are they ghosts?" panicked Humility, who was afraid of ghosts.

"Oh no, they aren't dead," he replied. "They're alive. They lost the imperfect physical bodies they had, when they died, but they themselves never actually died. Rather, they immediately received new physical bodies, in Heaven."

"Where's Heaven located then?" asked Humility.

"All over," he replied. "Other planets; other galaxies, and other dimensions. These blessed heroes of faith have come to see you. This entire field is a clean zone, which means that nothing anyone does, besides the wedding, can influence them. They are completely redeemed, which means that imperfection cannot touch them. You are not completely redeemed and won't be until you, also, lose your current physical body and receive a new perfect one. However, this wedding is redeemed, so they can witness it without being influenced by anything imperfect."

"Wow, I'm honored," said Humility.

"Yes, you are," said Dancer.

"What I meant is that you are honored, not me," she said, almost forgetting that he is God.

"It's alright, trust me, we are both honored," said Dancer.

The next thing to happen took the breath away from Humility, literally. A bright light exploded over the crowd, but there was no sound. They observed the light pulsating from God, and within the light was Humility, being cleansed by the light and renewed. Then, Dancer took her by the arms and began swinging her around as the crowd of heroes clapped a rhythmic beat to their wedding dance.

Then, Dancer placed a golden crown of jewels on Humility's head, and the crowd of heroes congratulated her as Dancer declared, "I give you, Queen Humility." After the wedding ceremony was over, Dancer walked Humility down the path that went underneath the river (the one that she saw when first in the labyrinth). As they came back to the beginning, they saw Pastor Guidance on the other side of the river, still standing still as a statue, on the other side of the entrance doorway.

"Why is he like that?" asked Humility.

"Because everything you are doing in the labyrinth is happening while no time has gone by in the rest of the world," said Dancer. "When you cross over the doorway, it will seem to Pastor Guidance that you never went anywhere. He might even ask you why you haven't gone in."

"I see, well, that's interesting, isn't it?" said Humility.

"It is," said Dancer. "Goodbye, Humility, in this form at least, for now. My Spirit is always with you. Just call my name, and we will continue our conversation about what you will be doing to start a spiritual revolution in the City of Spirituality."

"I will," said Humility. "Thank you, Dancer. Glory and honor to you, my Lord Jesus. My dearest eternal husband. My Creator; my God."

Chapter Eleven

The Showdown

It was almost noon on Saturday when Modesty arrived with her new boyfriend (Courtesy), to Virgil's Spiritual Coffee Shop. They were meeting up with Ambition, Comfort, and Conspiracy, to catch up on life and gossip about everything going on in the City of Spirituality. In fact, they couldn't have done it at a better time, because there were a lot of new and unusual things happening in the city. Ambition and Comfort are girls, and two of Modesty's friends from high school. Conspiracy is Comfort's boyfriend. They all got their coffee's, sat down at a table, and introduced each other to Courtesy (who was new to the group).

"Have you guys been following what's been going on, lately?" said Conspiracy.

"Do you mean with the Shame Enforcement Officers?" asked Ambition.

"That's all he talks about anymore," said Comfort. "He thinks something big is about to happen."

"Like what?" said Courtesy.

"Well, for starters, someone has challenged the Shame Enforcement Officers," said Conspiracy.

"Don't people challenge the Shame Enforcement Officers all the time?" asked Modesty.

"People resist them, but no one has ever challenged them," said Conspiracy.

"What's the difference?" said Ambition.

"Anyone can resist them, but they have no chance of changing what's coming, which is to be shamed," said Conspiracy. "But there are whispers of a rebellion. Someone has formed a group to fight back."

"What group?" said Courtesy. "We haven't heard of a rebellion."

"Seriously," said Comfort. "It's been all over the news. Everyone's talking about it."

"Not everyone," said Modesty.

"I've heard it's called the Children of the Labyrinth," said Ambition. "People say it was started by a girl our age. She found people to join her in standing against the Shame Enforcement Officers."

"But why would anyone want to mess with those guys?" said Courtesy. "We've seen them in action, and no one wants to get shamed; it's horrible."

"You saw someone get shamed?" asked Comfort. "Who was it?"

"It was Humility," said Modesty. "Actually, she was shamed twice."

"No way," said Ambition. "Not our Humility."

"Yes," said Modesty.

"Why?" asked Comfort.

"She broke the laws of social status by extending her spiritual authority above another man," said Modesty.

"Why would she do that?" asked Comfort.

"I don't really know," said Modesty. "Well, I kind of do. The first time, she suggested that God was something other than what a member of the City Council said he was, in front of a crowd, and soon after she was shamed. The second time, a Spiritually wise man called her a spiritual maggot, and she disagreed. For that, they shamed her a second time."

"But you don't know why she decided to break the law?" said Conspiracy.

"No," said Modesty.

"I'm sure we've all wanted to disagree with a spiritual leader, but I never found it worth being shamed," said Conspiracy.

"When did that happen?" asked Ambition.

"About two weeks ago," said Modesty.

"And what has she been doing since then?" asked Conspiracy.

"I don't know," returned Modesty.

"I wonder," said Conspiracy.

"You wonder what?" said Comfort.

"Well, this rumor of a rebellion started when word got out on the streets that a girl stood up to three Shame Enforcement Officers. Apparently, she followed them to a secluded park in the city and attacked them," said Conspiracy.

"I heard they tried to shame her, but instead, she shamed them," said Ambition.

"My sister's boyfriend, who is a Shame Enforcement Officer, told me that the officers who were attacked reported that this girl had magical powers," said Comfort.

"Sounds like a fairytale to me," said Courtesy. "Listen, we've seen what the Shame Enforcement Officers can do. No girl can do anything to them."

"They have powers too," said Modesty. "They can curse you if they want. They did it to Humility."

"Yes, but haven't you felt the increasing tension in the city this past week," said Conspiracy. "The Shame Enforcement Officers are nervous. Something or someone has made them nervous."

"Yeah, they have been shaming more people than ever before," said Comfort. "Anyone who even hints at nothing but complete loyalty to the city and the laws of social status, well, they get shamed, even if they didn't actually break the law."

"Then maybe we shouldn't be talking about it in public," said Modesty.

"I agree," said Courtesy. "We can't take the risk."

"Forget the Shame Enforcement Officers," said Ambition. "There are other similar stories that have nothing to do with them. Have you guys heard about that group of college students who were found roaming the city like zombies? The police confronted them and discovered they were completely non-responsive. They were taken to a mental hospital and treated for extreme PTSD."

"Post-traumatic stress disorder?" asked Modesty. "From what?"

"That's just it," said Ambition. "No one knew why, until finally, one of them snapped out of it and told the story. Apparently, these weren't just any old college students, but a gang called the Ridiculers. The police had been trying to catch them for years, and this girl confessed everything."

"Yes, but what traumatized them?" asked Conspiracy.

"They were confronted by a girl, who used magic on them, and somehow got into their minds. They called her a witch," said Ambition.

"Okay, but what does she have to do with the Children of the Labyrinth?" asked Courtesy.

"She's the leader and founder," said Conspiracy.

"This is all just rumors," said Modesty.

"Maybe, but I wonder," said Conspiracy.

"Here we go again," said Comfort. "What do you wonder?"

"I think Humility is the girl," said Conspiracy.

"Wait, you think Humility stood up to the Shame Enforcement Officers, bewitched the Ridiculers, and formed a rebellion called the Children of the Labyrinth?" asked Modesty.

"Why not?" said Conspiracy.

"You're out of your mind," said Modesty.

"Yeah," said Conspiracy. "Where is she, then? Has anyone seen her in the past two weeks? Since then, this mysterious girl has started a revolution. Does anyone else find that a little strange?"

"No, I haven't seen her, but I think you're crazy," said Modesty.

"No, it makes sense," said Comfort.

"Right, it could be her, if the rumors are true," said Ambition.

"I can't believe you guys," said Modesty. "Humility would never do those things."

"Think about it," said Courtesy. "We saw her get shamed, worse than I thought was possible. Who has more of a reason to stand against the Shame Enforcement Officers than Humility? Maybe she is the one doing it."

"She's my best friend," said Modesty. "I know her better than anyone. She would never do that. You're wrong. They are just rumors, anyway."

Their conversation was interrupted by a commotion going on in the streets. Crowds of people were moving toward the city center, which was only two blocks away. Modesty, Courtesy, Ambition, Comfort, and Conspiracy all got up from their table and stepped outside to get a closer look. They saw hundreds of people coming out of their apartments, out of shops and businesses, and gathering in the street to march toward the same direction. Men, women, children; all were curious what was going on. The word was spreading fast. Something big was going on in the city center.

"What's happening?" Courtesy asked someone in the crowd.

"The Council of Spirituality is in the city square," he said, and at this Modesty, Courtesy, Ambition, Comfort, and Conspiracy went the same directions as everyone else. When they arrived, they saw the twelve council members standing on a stage, with a hundred Shame Enforcement Officers between them and the crowd. Also, among them were various other police officers.

"This law breaker was caught writing these words, and desecrating our great City of Spirituality," said the Chief Council Member. He was pointing to a young girl, who looked around 13 years old, and was kneeling on the stage, with her head hung low. Then he pointed to painted letters on a nearby building wall; which read, "The revolution of the Children of the Labyrinth."

"Do you know what it says," continued the Chief. "It says a revolution is coming. This is a lie. There is no revolution. The Children of the Labyrinth is finished. We will destroy them, if we must. I promise you that. Such outlaw behavior will not be tolerated. This young girl shall be made an example of. She will be shamed, right here in front of you all."

Then, three Shame Enforcement Officers came onto the stage and stood around the girl. "Do your worst," said the Chief. "Strip her, beat her, and curse her."

"Stop," shouted a voice from within the crowd, and like magic, all the people around her moved away, so that she could easily be seen. It was Humility.

"Who are you?" shouted the Chief. "How dare you interrupt a shaming."

"I will do what I must. There will be no more shaming's. My name is Humility, leader of the Children of the Labyrinth," she said. Suddenly, the crowd moved away, but some people stayed. It was again, just like magic, because the people who moved away seemed to do it by someone else's power.

Those who didn't move, shouted, "We are the Children of the Labyrinth."

"Chief," shouted Humility. "These are my terms. You and the entire council of the City of Spirituality will surrender all authority over to the Children of the Labyrinth. The Shame Enforcement Officers will immediately stand-down and disband."

"And why would we do that?" the Chief screamed.

"Because we have the Spirit, or rather, the Spirit has us, and not even you should be so bold to challenge the Spirit of God," Humility shouted back. "He is in us and we are in him. He possesses us like a hurricane. He made everything. What chance do you think you have against him?"

"It's not him but you who we see here," shouted the Chief. "We do not fear your invisible God. You will be shamed most severe for this. Shame her; shame all of them."

The leader of the Shame Enforcement Officers heard this command and responded with a "yes sir."

However, as they approached the Children of the Labyrinth, it wasn't resistance they met, but outstretched arms. The first SEO to grab a member of the COTL could do nothing. The COTL were each putting a hand on a shoulder of all the officers. The hand gave out an electric like energy that warmed the body of the person it was touching. Every Shame Enforcement Officer was suddenly on the ground, laughing. The COTL finished walking through the crowd after they had touched everyone who they could tell was on the side of the Council.

Looking around, Humility could see every SEO and council member laughing hysterically. They would continue laughing like that for several months. And just like that, it was all over. The council was finished, the Shame Enforcement Officers were finished, and the government authority of the City of Spirituality was now under the control of the Children of the Labyrinth.

As you can probably imagine, Modesty was shocked. It all happened so fast. She couldn't believe it. Looking at Humility, she recognized her, but barely. She looked so different. Modesty tried to get closer to get Humility's attention, but by now the city square had become extremely crowded, and Modesty could hardy get anywhere in it. Everyone was cheering for Humility and the Children of the Labyrinth. In the next several minutes, followed by many hours and days, a weeklong celebration exploded on every block in the city.

Chapter Twelve

The Last Chapter

"Who is it?" said Humility, from the inside of her apartment, after she heard a knock on the front door. It had been a week since the showdown at the city square.

"It's me," said Modesty.

"What do you want?" asked Humility, still not opening the door.

"Are we not best friends?" replied Modesty. At this, Humility wanted to remind Modesty that she left her to be shamed again, but just as she was about to say it, she saw an image of Dancer in her mind. He was smiling, and from this, all the anger was suddenly gone.

"Come on in," said Humility, as she opened the door.

"Thanks," returned Modesty.

"I wasn't sure you still wanted to be friends, after everything that's happened," said Humility.

"Of course I do," said Modesty. "I don't really know what has happened. I know rumors, and I saw you overthrow the Council of Spirituality and the Shame Enforcement Officers, but I don't know what really happened. Is it true? Are you the leader of the Children of the Labyrinth?"

"Well, I suppose after you know the truth about me, you can decide then if you still want to be friends," said Humility.

"I will be your friend, no matter what," returned Modesty, but Humility gave her a suspicious look.

"You're not a prisoner of my friendship. You're not bound to me in any way," said Humility. "Let me tell you the truth, and then you can decide, and I will understand if you don't want to be friends anymore."

"Alright," said Modesty. "If you insist."

"The truth then," said Humility.

"The truth," replied Modesty.

"I met God," said Humility. They both sat down on the couch. Modesty didn't know what to say. She didn't know what that had to do with the Children of the Labyrinth.

"What does that mean?" asked Modesty.

"It means, I am a Christian," returned Humility.

"I don't understand. Is this connected to what's been going on?" asked Modesty.

"Yes, because it was God who told me to do what I did. He gave me the power to do it," explained Humility.

"Okay, but what exactly did you do? Are you now leader of the City of Spirituality?" asked Modesty.

"Heavens no. I don't want to do that. I couldn't if I wanted to," said Humility. "I met people who had the same experience as me, Christians who had been in the labyrinth, so I asked them if they would be willing to join me in starting a spiritual revolution; on God's orders. Naturally, on his orders, they said yes and called themselves the Children of the Labyrinth. I never meant for that to happen, and I certainly never meant to be seen as a leader."

"What's the labyrinth?" asked Modesty.

"It's a place where people go to meet God and get rid of their burdens," said Humility.

"So, you really believe in this Christian stuff?" asked Modesty.

"Yes, I do, because I've actually seen him. I talk to him. I know him very well," responded Humility.

"Who?" returned Modesty.

"Jesus," said Humility. "He's God. No one else is God, just him. But he goes by Dancer whenever we talk."

"Are you still with the Children of the Labyrinth? Are they

now governing the city?" asked Modesty, purposely ignoring what Humility just said, because she didn't know how to respond.

"Yes, but only unofficially," said Humility. "We elected leaders, and they are now forming the new political structure for the City of Spirituality, but I wanted nothing to do with it. I don't want to do that kind of thing."

"What do you want to do?" asked Modesty.

"Well. I tried going back to the ice-cream shop and seeing if I still had a job, but they hired someone else. I've got a little money saved up. Maybe I'll move back in with my mom and go to Bible College," said Humility.

"Really," said Modesty. "You're serious about this religious stuff, aren't you?"

"Yes, I am. Does that bother you?" asked Humility.

"No, it's just surprising," said Modesty.

The two of them kept talking until Humility had told Modesty everything. It took a while, but Modesty was a good audience, and by dinner they were finished. When Modesty had gone, Humility wondered what this all meant for her future. What kind of life would she have in the City of Spirituality? Would she be able to go on living without being noticed by very many people, or would she have to live with celebrity status? She didn't want it, and she would avoid it if she could.

She wondered what God wanted her to do with her life. Does he want her to be well known in the City of Spirituality? Does he want her to be a leader or a politician? She was curious, so she simply asked him. He told her that she would do great things for him, and that there are many ways to accomplish things without having to be a celebrity or a politician. He affirmed her idea to get a Bible education, but not from just any Bible school. There was one particular school that he recommended as the best one for her life's purpose.

"And what purpose is that?" she asked.

"Well, I am sorry, but I won't tell you the details about your future; not now anyway. What I can tell you, however, is that it will be very miraculous, and very revolutionary," said Dancer.

"Like what we did to the Council of Spirituality and the Shame Enforcement Officers?" asked Humility.

"I think that when it's all over, you will view that showdown as a rather small event in the big picture of things. What you will accomplish will shock even me," said Dancer.

"That's difficult to believe," said Humility.

"Yes, but most things I say are difficult to believe at first, until you become familiar with what's happening. That's the nature of faith," said Dancer.

THE END

Printed in the United States
By Bookmasters